Paul
10/24/03

L'ART DE VIVRE

L'ART DE VIVRE

A Fable about Paris in the 1930s

Paul J. Schwartz

iUniverse, Inc.
New York Lincoln Shanghai

L'Art de Vivre
A Fable about Paris in the 1930s

iUniverse, Inc.

For information address:
iUniverse, Inc.
2021 Pine Lake Road, Suite 100
Lincoln, NE 68512
www.iuniverse.com

Although the characters in this novel are fictitious, Richard Rosendale was inspired by the work of an American sculptor living in Paris during the 1970s, and Claudine and Olivier d'Anglade owe much to two characters briefly sketched in Georges Perec's 1978 novel, *Life a User's Manual*.

ISBN: 0-595-28733-6 (pbk)
ISBN: 0-595-65839-3 (cloth)

Printed in the United States of America

Prologue

On the Plateau St. Michel, just at the point where Departmental Route 2 enters the southern French village of Vence, stands an imposing four-story stucco house, whose large, walled terrace and balconied bedrooms overlook not only the winding highway, but also the charming orange-tiled private houses with terraced gardens, as well as the embarrassingly ugly utilitarian apartment complexes built over the last half century into the southern slope of the Maritime Alps, to absorb hungrily the powerful rays of the Mediterranean sun. In the early part of the twentieth century, this former mountain retreat of a Monacan banker had been renovated as a luxury hotel, which then ran into hard times during the First World War, was abandoned during the 1920s, and by the early '30s was in desperate shape. However, new owners, rumored to be backed by the resources of a rich Parisian banker, took over late in the summer of 1936. They quickly restored the building's twenty hotel rooms and suites (two on the ground floor and six on each of the other levels), each elaborately decorated with brightly colored mosaic tiles and hand-painted wall designs featuring feathery motifs.

The hotel manager, a young Parisian woman named Martine, quickly won the admiration and respect of her Vençois neighbors and suppliers with her astute commercial judgment, her firmness and fairness in dealing with them, her cheerfulness and good will. The improvement she brought to the property helped boost the economy of the whole St. Michel neighborhood, as the rooms and apartments were nearly always filled with tourists coming from Germany, Holland and England, as well as from Paris, to enjoy the beauty, comfort, and spectacular surroundings of the Hôtel Miramar.

As unanimous and enthusiastic as the locals were in their appreciation of Martine, their expressions changed and their eyes rolled significantly when asked about her husband. He was seen little if at all, and his conversation usually consisted of monosyllabic or evasive answers in a pretty heavily accented French. He seemed to go out of his way to avoid conversation. Most assumed he was German, and embarrassed by his nationality. Martine spoke little of him, but made it clear that he was the artistic presence behind the success of Miramar. His mosaics and wall motifs contributed heavily to the hotel's charm and reputation.

One of the nicer apartments, located on the top floor facing south, was rented in permanence to a middle-aged couple, Parisian art dealers who had recently opened a gallery in nearby Saint-Paul. Another luxurious apartment was rented permanently to an obviously wealthy but reclusive middle-aged gentleman with a distinguished beard and elegant dress, who usually appeared at the hotel after dark, pulling into the hotel's only garage space in a black Citroën. A third, more modest apartment was permanently occupied by a younger man, reputed to be a writer, who called himself André. The clicking sound of a typewriter could be heard emanating from his room at all hours…

CHAPTER 1

The large apartment buildings on the rue Barbet de Jouy in the fashionable section of Paris's seventh *arrondissement* near the Ministry of Agriculture overlook the gardens of the Musée Rodin. The corner penthouse of No. 73, rue Barbet de Jouy, occupied from early March 1922, until May of 1936 by the Baron and Baroness d'Anglade, has a large wrought iron-railed terrace which extends along the back of the eighth floor at a point just north of "The Thinker." In early spring, the outer edge of the terrace catches the first rays of the morning sun, and by mid-morning basks in enough warmth to support several pots of geraniums and dwarf palms. Three doors along the west side of the building give access respectively to the kitchen, dining room and master bedroom. It is on this terrace at a massive wood and iron table that M. le Baron Olivier d'Anglade sat at 8:30 on the morning of April 11, 1936, immaculately dressed and groomed but without a suit coat. The weather had been excellent, extraordinary really for any time of year, nearly unprecedented sunshine and warmth for mid-April.

The Baron was in his fifty-second year; his thinning hair and expanded waistline did not mar his remarkable good looks. The elegance of his silk dress shirt and gold cuff links announced a man of wealth and taste. He rang once the polished silver bell by his already set place at the table, and continued reading *Le Figaro*. Within seconds, Mme Brunot, who had served the Baron and his wife since the second month following their establishment in their rue de Jouy apartment, entered respectfully.

"Would you like your usual breakfast, M. le Baron?"

"Yes, Mme Brunot, but don't serve me any more of those peach preserves my mother-in-law brought us. Strawberry, please."

"Certainly, M. le Baron. Will Mme la Baronne be breakfasting with you?"

"What? Oh, yes, I suppose so."

"Then, I'd better bring the peach also."

"If you like."

Even before Mme Brunot had finished her tactful, but firm negotiations with the Baron on the potentially divisive issue of preserves, he had returned earnestly to the morning paper. Several articles attracted his attention. Mildly interested in the front page's sensational headline about mechanical failures aboard the Hindenburg, which had nearly caused a major disaster, he was much more absorbed in the account of the newly published English/French joint communiqué expressing concern with Germany's recent aggressive posturing, and an editorial condemning the growing strength of extreme left wing political movements in the industrial suburbs surrounding Paris. Among the interesting *faits divers* of the day, including a minor train crash, the explosion of a gas truck outside of Angoulême, a robbery and an attempted murder, the Baron found himself unusually engrossed in a brief account of the theft from the museum in Segovia, Spain, of four valuable paintings by Dürer and Rembrandt. The principal suspect was an elegantly dressed individual who on the preceding Sunday had spent several hours in the room where they were exhibited, and who was suspecting of having had reproduced a key to the outside door.

Another article, buried behind these more obviously appealing stories, especially attracted his attention. But before he could make much progress in it, Claudine d'Anglade entered from the bedroom wearing an elegant dressing gown, her hair down. Despite her forty-eight years, and even without her usual cosmetic artistry, Claudine was stunningly blond, fit and beautiful.

"Good morning, Olivier."

He returned her greeting mechanically without looking up. She ignored his bad manners, and pressed on, trying patiently to get his attention: "You were out late last night…I say, you were out late last night."

"Yes, playing whist with the Attorney-General and two highly placed members of his staff."

"I wasn't prying. I say I wasn't prying."

"Of course not, we don't pry."

There was nothing unusual about Claudine's difficulty in engaging her husband in conversation. What was unusual was her persistence. It was as if on this particular morning, when in fact Olivier was more than moderately absorbed in a newspaper article of particular importance for his career, out of spite, loneliness or curiosity, she were single-mindedly intent on penetrating his consciousness, forcing herself uncharacteristically upon him.

"And who were these highly placed members of the Attorney-General's staff?"

Having absorbed most of the information in the *Figaro* article and sensing the strength of his wife's determination, Olivier politely folded his paper, took off his glasses and smiled at Claudine, "Jean Beaulieu and Frédéric Valençais. If you really must know, Frédéric and I were partners, and we won two thousand francs."

Unconsciously, Claudine started at the mention of Valençais. Her surprise turned to a smile reflecting amusement and a hint of triumph, "Ah, yes, Frédéric Valençais."

"An old friend of yours if I remember correctly."

"Now, who's prying?"

"We don't pry."

Sincerely amused by both her recollections of Frédéric Valençais and her husband's graciousness, Claudine pursued her advantage, "That was almost ten years ago, anyway. Is Frédéric doing well?"

"Quite well. Having faithfully served the party in the senate, he's now in line for a ministerial appointment. He has an exciting future."

"He's had an exciting past."

"Really? I wouldn't know."

"I would."

Mme Brunot returned at this point carrying a generous breakfast with both peach and strawberry preserves; Olivier served himself and returned to his paper. Claudine was miffed to be so quickly dismissed.

"You seem terribly absorbed. What's so interesting?"

Once again yielding politely to his wife's almost reckless forcefulness, Olivier refolded his paper, this time a little more deliberately, "Speculation about the imminent shake-up in the organization of the Interior Ministry. I have been watching this develop, even sowing a few rumors, as it may be my last chance to rise above the certainly not humble but still constraining position of Chief Magistrate of the Paris Court."

Delighted to have her husband's confidence, Claudine tried a little semi-sincere flattery, "I am sure, my dear, that deGrael is eager to have among his inner circle of advisors the sharpest legal mind in all of France…"

"Really, Claudine, the sharpest legal mind…?"

Claudine, despite her good humor, was still mildly indignant at her husband's naive vanity, "You told me so yourself, my dear."

Olivier went on at length explaining to Claudine the opportunities and the obstacles. A high-ranking position in the Interior Ministry required, in addition to good connections and appropriate experience, an astute political savoir-faire. The old-timers in the Interior Ministry were suspicious of "fine legal minds." Political considerations often outweighed legal punctiliousness, even in an enlightened, populist era, such as France in the 1930s, and Olivier had to persuade deGrael and his advisors that his command of tact and diplomacy and his awareness of the subtleties of political discourse were as finely hewn as his sensitivity to the law. The Police in France was, and always has been, somewhat embarrassed by the law. So, for a magistrate to rise to a position of power within the Interior Ministry would be completely unthinkable were it not for Olivier's special friendship with deGrael, dating back to their lycée days together in Bordeaux. Without deGrael's firm support he would certainly have to be content to continue to spend the rest of his public life at the beck and call of the most daring criminals in the land.

Claudine, suddenly awake to the potential for excitement in her life, and the possibility of a role for herself in her husband's ambition, did not hesitate to offer herself: "Is that why the invitation to dine with the deGraels tonight has you so excited?"

"Oh, you haven't forgotten?"

"You certainly haven't given me the slightest opportunity to forget it. We are to be ready to leave at precisely 7:25. The car will be downstairs at 7:30. I am to wear my burgundy evening gown and diamond pendant; your charcoal tuxedo and ruffled shirt are to be pressed and ready by 6:30. Did I leave anything out?"

"The truffles from Fauchon?"

"They'll be delivered before we arrive."

"Good."

"As you can see, I still carry out nobly some of my conjugal obligations…"

"Yes, of course."

"…and given the opportunity, I would still be able to satisfactorily meet others."

Mme Brunot's re-entrance to pour more coffee interrupted the disapproving look which was all that Olivier permitted himself in response to Claudine's playfully expressed but nonetheless deeply felt and frequently expressed pique. While the d'Anglades had maintained in their very public social life the appearance of contentment and devotion in marriage which for more than ten years had been real, their relationship had by now been seriously eroded.

Olivier was the first to stray; in their twelfth year of marriage, he began a series of somewhat squalid affairs with women beneath him socially, some "not even pretty" as Claudine complained (but only to him). He made no attempt to shield Claudine from his adventures; in fact, it was she who often found herself in the absurd position of hiding her husband's transgressions from the rest of the world, and especially from her mother and their daughters.

Claudine's revenge amounted to two dalliances, purposely chosen from suitors within their own world (one the fortunate Valençais), to which she yielded with the desperate hope of drawing her husband back to her bedroom.

Mme Brunot interrupted Olivier's reproachful look, "Excuse me, Mme la Baronne, but I almost forgot to tell you that your daughter, Mme Denonceaux, called late yesterday afternoon, just before I went upstairs.

"Did she leave a message?"

"Just that she had called…and that she and M. Denonceaux will be staying the weekend at Antibes."

Claudine thanked Mme Brunot and waited for her to leave before exclaiming to Olivier reburied in his paper, "Well, how about that? I had thought that we were going to have both Daphné's and Nicole's family this weekend with us in Burgundy, and they've both cancelled out. I got a note from Daphné yesterday, saying that Georges had injured his back falling from his horse. Needs to stay in bed five days, the poor fellow. So it looks like we'll have the whole house to ourselves. I say, Olivier, what do you suppose the two of us can do for a whole weekend by ourselves in our isolated country house in Burgundy?"

"I certainly don't have the faintest idea. I was looking forward to playing some golf with Georges and Lucien. Maybe we should stay in town."

Olivier plunged back into his newspaper, consciously avoiding the taunts he knew he had inspired, "So that you'll not miss your friends here!" As Olivier cowered behind his paper, Claudine went on, her anger turning to a desperate desire to placate, "Olivier, will you please tell your friends that they don't have to hang up when I answer the phone. I am perfectly capable of taking messages. And I am discreet…I suppose I could invite mother to join us. No, that really wouldn't suit either of us. I can assure you that I find her monologues and harangues as tiring as you do, dear. Do you have a busy day, Olivier? Olivier, what are your plans for the day?"

"Oh, the usual routine. Several meetings. I have to be in court from three to five."

"An exciting case?"

"A very dull affair, really: a man murdered his wife because she wouldn't let him enjoy his breakfast and newspaper in peace. Seems to me there was a mother-in-law mixed up in it somewhere, too."

"Very funny. Will you be lunching at home?"

"Better tell Mme Brunot not to count on me. Roger Sanchon and Philippe Laurent are expecting me to join them, I believe."

Claudine accepted Olivier's evasiveness with good grace "Oh, I see. Are you interested in my day? Well, you'll be glad to know that I will call on Mme Dumesnil this afternoon. For months she's been trying to get me to drop in on her Wednesday afternoon circle, and I've never gone. It's so tiresome to have to go all the way out to St.-Germain, but she has insisted on sending a car in for me, and I just got tired of making excuses. So, I will drink tea and eat cookies and hear all of the latest scandals and gossip of the fashion industry. Really, what could be less interesting than selling clothing? But don't worry, Olivier, (who shows no worry or even interest) I will be back in plenty of time to prepare for the deGrael's dinner. Olivier...Olivier, whom else have they invited?"

"I believe it will just be the five of us?"

"Five?"

"Michel, Geneviève, and Geneviève's deaf mother."

"Oh, yes, I had forgotten about Mme Grabois. What a frightful bore she is!"

"I am sure that Michel will more than compensate for his mother-in-law's dullness."

"Now, Olivier, you know very well that I have never responded to Michel's outrageous flirting. Would it help your career if I did?"

"I don't imagine that it would. No, just be charming and discreet, the perfect wife of the perfect diplomat."

Olivier rang twice the dainty silver bell at his place. After a pause, M. Brunot, the perfect complement to Mme Brunot, entered. "You rang, M. le Baron?"

"Brunot, help me with my jacket, please." The servant took a suit coat from the bedroom, helped Olivier put it on, and then very ceremoniously whisked it, adjusted his tie, and bowed.

Olivier smiled to his wife, started to leave, then came back, "You won't forget about the tuxedo and shirt?"

"Of course not. Good-bye, Olivier." D'Anglade smiled again as he left. Claudine and M. Brunot followed Olivier towards the door; Brunot took leave of her after determining that she had no further use of his services. Claudine decided to call her daughter Nicole before bathing, to plead with her for at least part of the weekend. She sensed that this was both inappropriate and certain to fail, but needed nonetheless to register her disappointment.

After a long static-filled delay, the operator succeeded in completing the call from Paris to Antibes. "Hello, Nicole…this is your mother."

"Yes, mother, Mme Brunot gave you my message?"

"Yes, she gave me the message this morning. Dear, is there any chance that you and Lucien could make it for even part of the weekend?"

"No, I'm afraid not. Lucien has accepted an invitation to spend the weekend with the Grandvilles. He was very apologetic because he knew how much I wanted to be in Burgundy with you…I mean, we both did, but it's an invitation that I'm sure you understand we couldn't turn down."

"Oh, I see…Well, we certainly don't want to interfere with your plans…It's just that Daphné has canceled out too, and your father is suggesting that we stay in town. And I was so looking forward to getting out of Paris, and of course to seeing you again."

"We'll definitely come up the weekend of the 27th."

"Well, then, we'll count on you for that weekend…My love to Lucien. Good-bye, dear."

Claudine hung up, sadly, "Another depressing weekend in Paris."

CHAPTER 2

The Friedland Gallery was located about a mile east of the d'Anglade apartment on the Rue de Seine about two hundred yards south of the Institut Français. It was a small and undistinguished gallery to which most passers-by failed to give a second glance as they scurried along to the market or the more prestigious galleries up the street. On that same glorious April day, at mid-afternoon, Jacques and Joanne Friedland with the help of Richard Rosendale and Martine Lenouet, were preparing the gallery for the opening of Rosendale's exhibit "Feathered Friends". The gallery was littered with opened boxes and packing material. There were about a dozen of Rosendale's avant-garde sculptures, dreary and boring pieces with feathers attached, around the ground floor of the gallery. As Joanne, was about to remove one of two sculptures from a crowded table, Richard stopped her with a frantic gesture:

"*Non, non, Joanne, il faut que ces deux restent ensemble.*" Richard, an American, spoke correct French with a strong accent.

Joanne objected that the two sculptures together on the same table looked crowded, and the other side of the gallery still seemed a little bare.

"This is no time to be hung up on symmetry, Joanne. Alpha and Romeo were created as a pair. Alpha was of course the first piece of the series. I was tempted to call his mate Beta, but decided to go with a free associative, masculine pairing: not Alpha and Beta, not Romeo and Juliet, but Alpha and Romeo, distinct yet surely greater than the sum of their parts. But, you know, you're right, they are too crowded there. They lack *espace vital*. Alpha Romeo on a small table! No! Let's put them over here, suspended, with Alpha hovering over Romeo."

Joanne got the wire and cutters to hang them as instructed. With Richard watching nervously over her shoulder, she inserted a small eye hook at either end of the sculpture, balancing it so that it would hang upright. When, after twenty minutes, it was finally suspended to Richard's satisfaction, Joanne could not resist a mild expression of impatience:

"If you keep this up, Richard, we'll still be rearranging the exhibit long after our guests have left."

"So what? Art isn't static. Do you think that I gave these sculptures feathers so that they would always sit in one place. The feathers give them an inertia blasting freedom which requires them to be always moving, always in flight."

Martine, who had tried to be helpful without getting in the way by carefully unpacking the sculptures and lining them up against the back wall of the gallery, asked if there were any left outside in the van.

Joanne answered that she had brought in the last three, "Pyro, Gaston and Adonis."

Richard exploded in semi-serious indignation, "That's not Adonis, it's Orion! Curious confusion. The hunter, not the lover. Both manifest latent virility, it is true (pointing to a suggestive protuberance), but this piece represents the destructive aggressiveness of the hunter, adorned with his trophies, feathers plucked from his vanquished victims. The plumage worn by Adonis upstairs in the loft is more decorative, more seductive, but indicative at the same time of a potential trophy."

As the delightful warm and sunny afternoon gradually gave way to evening clouds, the work went on, interrupted by Richard's frequent dissertations on the meaning of various pieces in the exhibit, to which Joanne and Martine listened with patience and occasional bemusement. Jacques interrupted one of Richard's longer expositions with a less than polite but still business-like question, "Is it too early to set out the wine bottles, Joanne?"

Joanne noted the barely disguised irritation in her husband's voice, checked her watch and decided to push, "We'd better make sure we know where all the sculptures are going first. Richard, don't you think we should bring down two or three from the loft? Lots of our guests will never even get up there, and it's a shame to leave some of your best pieces where…"

Richard reacted with exaggerated horror: "I know this is hard for you to understand, Joanne, but these feathered sculptures really do have a life of their own. How can I stop Pegasus and Pterodactyl from seeking solace in the loft? Tamed by me, deprived of their natural environments, they instinctively seek out higher elevations and…"

Joanne interrupted before any further damage could be done to their friendship: "Go ahead and set out the refreshments, Jacques, all except the champagne which we'll want to keep chilled until the last minute."

Richard offered to accompany Jacques into the cellar to help select the appropriate bottles to accompany his exhibit "something light of course, but distinctive, and…" Martine who had been watching and listening with a mixture of admiration and anxiety approached Joanne, seeking to reassure herself and at the same time to express sympathy and appreciation.

"Do you really think we'll have over a hundred people?"

"That's what we usually count on. People know that the Friedland Gallery is highly selective and trust us not to disappoint them when we exhibit a new artist."

"Richard isn't exactly new."

"He is new to the wealthy collectors who come to us. This is his first exhibit in several years. No one remembers his 1932 exhibit at the Galerie des Saints-Pères."

Jacques, who had overheard the last comment by his wife, entered at that moment with several bottles, muttering, "That's something to be grateful for," and re-exited before Martine and Joanne had time to record their indignation.

Joanne went on optimistically, "The fact that he's been teaching for several years should help too. I expect many of his former students to drop in tonight."

"And the press?"

Joanne admitted that Richard did not have enough of a reputation to draw the more influential art critics, but added that their mutual friend Raymond Crosatier would come out of friendship and try to get a small piece into the next day's *Figaro*.

"I can't tell you how grateful we are, Joanne, for your support. It's so hard to sell anything unless you're exhibited, and Richard isn't very good at selling himself."

"We walk a thin line, Martine, trying to make a living while at the same time trying to promote beginning artists. We've had a good spring, so we can afford to take a chance on Richard."

At this point, Richard and Jacques came back up with more bottles and glasses. Martine, who remembered Richard's last disastrous exhibit, was convinced they were overdoing it, "Oh my, looks like enough for a huge crowd."

Jacques agreed but nonetheless anticipated an evening of fun and laughter, "Or more likely, a small crowd having a wonderful time."

The notion of gayety set Richard off again, "Gayety will be entirely appropriate amidst my 'Feathered Friends'. Feathers, laughter, lightness: effervescent bubbles of champagne accompanying my soaring sculptures, laughter rising with them. Oh, I hope our guests like my friends! I have been working on 'Feathered Friends' since last November. For six months I had produced nothing, following my breakdown…"

Richard broke off, noticing that all three listeners appeared uncomfortable at the reminder of the moderately severe breakdown which had briefly hospitalized him the previous spring.

"Oh, you don't have to be embarrassed about that. I'm not. I don't mind talking about my breakdown. In fact, my analyst says it's good for me to talk about it. You see, when faced with the meaninglessness of life on one hand, and the public's failure to appreciate my expression of that meaninglessness, well, I was severely depressed, suicidal in fact. But the one thing that kept me going, that kept me from throwing myself into the Seine, was my continuous belief in my ability to express all the dark feelings I had. Those dark feelings, the sense of despair and hopelessness which I feel when I see what is happening in the world, and which I have always expressed in my work, I decided to give to them a new face, a buoyant, optimistic, uplifting levity. And so in November I started putting feathers on my pieces. I first tried putting feathers on some of my older pieces. And then I began creating new pieces designed to resist feathers, pieces to which it seemed impossible to apply feathers—and then I put feathers on them, and feathery names too which contrast with the heavy burden of despair they at first carried."

Martine added her hope that the public would respond more appreciatively to Richard's optimistic art forms. Moving closer and embracing her clumsily, Richard added that Martine deserved a lot of credit for this new phase of his work. "She's been an important part of my recovery. Her encouragement and support have gotten me through lots of bad days. In fact the feathers were her idea, really…"

Over Martine's objection, Richard explained that the feathers were "my response to what you were trying to tell me about life, about how to see despair as possibility, really and fundamentally, to see death as potential life."

"Now, you know perfectly well that I never said anything like that, Richard."

"You kept telling me to keep my chin up…How better to do it than with feathers?"

Joanne suddenly noticed the hour, and rushed for her broom, "This is all very nice, but we're going to have people here in an hour, and this place doesn't look very good at all. Now, Richard, is this the final arrangement of the pieces?"

"Yes, this is the final arrangement—for now."

"Good, I guess that's the best I can hope for. So, let's clear the trash out of here, so I can start sweeping and dusting."

A flurry of activity ensued. Jacques, Martine and Richard stuffed packing material back into empty crates, and carted the crates into the back room, as Joanne dusted, swept and made final adjustments to the exhibit pieces.

Within minutes, the gallery had assumed an air of simple elegance which set off Richard's pieces to their best advantage. As they were about to complete their final inspection, the gallery door opened and in walked a tall, elegantly dressed gentleman with a moustache, a cane and a decidedly mischievous grin, Raymond Crosatier.

Joanne was the first to spot him, "Raymond, I'm so glad you've come." Richard and Martine echoed her greeting, "Yes, we all are!"

Raymond Crosatier was one of the first people Richard had met when he came to Paris in 1928. Although Raymond had been studying comparative literature at the Sorbonne, he had tended to socialize more readily with the Beaux-Arts students who, like Richard, frequented the cafés of Saint-Germain des Prés. Raymond had dreamed of a career as a writer and more easily identified with the Bohemian temperaments of the budding artists than with the more bourgeois aspirations of the literature students. He enjoyed the wild parties and creative pranks of the art students, and had been especially drawn to Richard's outgoing personality and frequently bombastic discourse. He admired Richard's persistent dedication to the arts, and felt keen frustration with his own decision to pursue a career in journalism.

As he entered, Raymond smiled with a mixture of irony and friendliness, "I hope you don't mind my coming a little early. I wanted to have a chance to view the exhibit without bumping into a lot of people."

Joanne solicitously reassured him: "Of course, Raymond. Is the *Figaro* really going to publish your critique?"

"Sort of."

"Sort of?"

Raymond smiled apologetically: "They've given me five centimeters."

Martine, Jacques and Joanne all groaned, "Five centimeters!"

"I know it's not much, but it will attract some attention." Trying to demonstrate a sincere interest, Raymond turned to Richard, "So, Richard, what can you tell me about your 'Feathered Friends'?"

"I really prefer to let them speak for themselves."

Raymond nods, "Oh, I see." and turned to Alpha and Romeo now suspended just above his head, "Let's see what these two birds have to say for themselves. Speak up, fellows, I can't hear you."

Martine jumped in, anticipating Richard's discomfort at Raymond's ironic disrespect, "Raymond, they are expressions of Richard's despair to which he has given wings."

"Winged despair, I see." Raymond read the title plates, "Alpha and Romeo. Sort of a mixed metaphor which yet stands on its own."

"Which soars on its own," Richard corrected him.

"Not unless Alpha Romeo has started making airplanes. Otherwise, they're most often seen going round and round in circles on a race track, making lots of noise, and incidentally money, but not really getting any-where."

Richard, somewhat offended by Raymond's mocking tone, asked bluntly, "Is that your judgment of my work?"

"They aren't going to make a lot of money, Richard."

"Of course not, but do you really think they're not going anywhere?"

Raymond, who used his bantering humor as a stalling tactic while he tried to form a studied judgment, did not really want to be offensive or discouraging. "I'm not sure yet. Let me look around a little more." He read the title of another sculpture resting squarely on a small table in the corner, "Gaston. A political allusion?"

"No, it's really a fairly obscure joke, the title that is. I don't even know the origin of the American phrase 'an Alphonse and Gaston act', but they're two characters each of whom waits for the other to go first. The joke here is there's no Alphonse."

Raymond obviously enjoyed the humor, "So not only is he not going anywhere, but he really has no reason not to."

"Yes, I suppose so."

Raymond pulled out a notebook and scribbled notes as he continued to look around and occasionally questioned Richard, "Besides feathers, what are your basic materials?"

Richard would have preferred not to dwell on the technical dimen-sions of his work, but was eager to accommodate the journalist, "All of the pieces are partially cast bronze, with a variety of other materials that I pick up."

Raymond muttered as he wrote, "Bronze, feathers and junk. And what kind of feathers?"

"Lots of pigeon feathers, but some I've bought: eagle, ostrich, even peacock."

"Good. Are there more upstairs?"

Joanne assured him that some of the better pieces were upstairs, and offered to accompany Richard and Raymond into the loft.

Martine's confidence had in no way been bolstered by the critic's breezy condescension. She took advantage of the move upstairs to seek reassurance from Jacques, "Oh, Jacques, I don't think he likes them."

Jacques tried to reassure her, "Even if he doesn't, he's still a good enough friend so he'll find something positive to write. Besides, you can't really tell with Raymond. He's always cynical and negative. He may really be loving this stuff."

"Are he and Richard really good friends?"

"When they were students, he and Richard shared an apartment."

"I know that, but can we really trust him?"

"I think so. He's got to be honest, no phony hype. He's got to watch out for his own reputation. But he's not the kind to try to build his reputation by trashing the work of a struggling artist, especially when that artist is a friend."

"And what about your customers, Jacques? Are they going to like his work? I'm so afraid that another failure would be more than Richard could take."

"You're really in love with him, aren't you?"

"Of course. But I also respect and admire him. I feel sorry for him too."

"Yeah, for people like Richard, there's no happiness, just an occasional freedom from pain."

"No, you're wrong, Jacques. That's not really Richard. He talks a lot about despair and depression, but he's really a lot of fun. Sometimes I think he talks that way because he thinks he's supposed to."

"You mean he's playing a role?"

"Yes, to some extent he wants to be the suffering artist. All that talk about his breakdown, for example. He enjoys exaggerating it. He did have some serious problems with the lack of acceptance of his work, but he's no brooding artist out of touch with his age. His breakdown was really just frustration with his lack of success. The only thing that really depresses Richard is his poverty. It bothers him when I give him money—not that I have a lot to give. But he really has practically no income now that most of his students have dropped him."

"His courses never have been very popular."

Martine nodded sadly, "Let's face it, Richard's a lousy teacher. How can you learn sculpture from someone who's always talking in terms of latent virility and potential trophies. Eventually the students realize that there's little relationship between fancy language and sculpture."

Jacques suddenly smiled, "You know you're right about his being a lot of fun. Yeah, I had forgotten that Richard really used to be a funny man. I remember him when he was a student at Beaux Arts, that's when I first met him. He used to pull some really crazy stunts, and we had some wild parties too."

"What kind of stunts?"

I guess the craziest was one Easter when he got a friend of his in Medical School to steal a cadaver…"

Martine interrupted, "I don't think I want to hear this…"

Jacques agreed, "Probably not. A lot of worshipers at Saint-Sulpice were very surprised when they entered the church that Easter morning and saw a crucifixion, that, uh…"

Martine interrupted again, "I'm glad that I didn't know him then. He's certainly mellowed a lot, but he still knows how to laugh and have a good time—and pull crazy stunts—when he's not wondering where his next meal is coming from."

Martine lowered her voice as Richard, Joanne and Raymond came down the spiral staircase from the loft. Richard's spirits had obviously improved as he laughingly grabbed Raymond's arm and exclaimed,

"No, no, Raymond, I can't let you buy them all before the exhibit opens. We have to have something here for my public to view."

Raymond chuckled, "OK. I forgot my checkbook anyway. But I'll be back as soon as the exhibit closes."

Jacques offered Raymond a glass of champagne, and went off to get a bottle from the refrigerator. Raymond eagerly accepted as Jacques brought in a bottle which he ceremoniously opened and poured glasses for everyone.

After the appropriate toasts, Raymond looked at his watch and observed, "I can't stay long. I have to get my story in. I was sort of tempted to write it before seeing the exhibit, but they don't like it anymore when you do that."

Richard blurted out, "Raymond, I can't stand the suspense any longer, what are you going to write?"

Raymond smiled, closed his eyes and announced, "I will write that I have visited the largest aviary within the Paris city limits, that the zoo keepers serve excellent champagne, and that considering the nature of the beasts exhibited therein, the smell really isn't that bad."

Richard grimaced, "Do you mean that the exhibit doesn't stink?"

"Is that what you want me to write: 'Richard Rosendale's new exhibit of sculptures at the Friedland Gallery does not stink!'"

"Really, Richard, I need to look over my notes, think about what I've seen and listen to the words that flow from my mind. You know, art criticism is also a form of personal expression. Can you tell me in advance what your next sculpture will look like? I mean in its details and overall expression? And can you predict in advance how it will be interpreted by different viewers?"

Richard was unwilling to let Raymond off the hook, "So, you're going to write an artistic ambiguous piece that even you won't know what it's supposed to say?"

"Richard, I don't know what I'm going to write. But I'd better do it soon before drinking too much of this wonderful stuff."

Joanne clasped Raymond's hand, "Thanks for coming by, Raymond. We appreciate your getting us coverage."

Raymond smiled, "You're certainly welcome. And lots of luck with the real critics, the ones with the money and inclination to buy art works. *Au revoir.*"

Richard sat down heavily as Raymond left the gallery, "With friends like that…"

Joanne tried to comfort him, "Now, Richard, you know he wants to help."

Richard as usual found solace in his own words, "Who cares anyway? Who cares what a contemporary art critic—and for that matter a contemporary public—think of my creations. Future generations will learn to love them. In a hundred years, visitors to the Grand Palais retrospective of my works—or to the Rosendale museum—will be saddened as they read of my short and miserable life, at the same time that they will be uplifted by the moving spectacle of dozens of my sculptures which, happier and less ephemeral than their creator, have gone forth through time as monuments to my sorrow and my creativity."

Joanne couldn't resist an attempt to bring him back to earth, "I hate to interrupt you with ephemeral banalities, Richard, but the ability of the four of us to eat and drink in the very near future depends to a great extent on what a contemporary critic and some hundred—I hope I'm not being too optimistic—representatives of the contemporary public think of your 'Feathered Friends' tonight."

Richard was sincerely contrite, "I'm sorry, Joanne. I am grateful for your going out on a limb like this for me—champagne and all. What we really all want is for two or three filthy rich collectors—who cares whether they be people of taste and distinction?—to come in here and fall in love with my 'Feathered Friends'. Then our future and the sculptures' future will be equally assured."

Joanne raised her half-full glass, "Here's to filthy rich collectors."

Jacques lifted his glass, "May they come in droves."

And Richard embraced Martine: "I'll drink to that!"

CHAPTER 3

❀

That evening, Claudine accompanied her husband to the deGrael's luxurious apartment on the rue des Mathurins with mixed feelings. She welcomed any chance to go out, to interrupt the cycle of boredom inside of which her life was inscribed. Her participation in her husband's ambition and the opportunity to see it played out in a semi-public setting created a certain excitement. But this was basically a business dinner, a required affair to which she was not invited but convened. She would play a role not of her own choosing. And it was not a particularly pretty role, since she would have to expose herself to Michel deGrael's unwanted gallantry. Not that Michel was particularly undesirable; his charm, position and obvious interest in Claudine were endearing. But she had long ago hardened herself against her husband's oldest friend and trusted mentor, so as not to complicate her life.

The ministerial car left them at the apartment entrance where an elegantly attired doorman greeted them and escorted them politely into the elevator. Michel deGrael himself, alerted by the doorman, was waiting for them as the elevator opened in front of their seventh floor penthouse, and before they knew it, Olivier and Claudine, Michel and Geneviève deGrael, and Geneviève's mother Mme Grabois were seated on plush divans in the apartment's intimate receiving room, drinking champagne, and talking about food.

Michel commented that in his estimation there were few places left in Paris where one can count on getting a good meal, as most of the hotels and restaurants pandered to the tastes of British and American tourists. "It seems that one eats well only at home."

Claudine countered that she still enjoyed dining at the Tour d'Argent, but Michel argued that even there, you know, it's not what it used to be. "One encounters all sorts of foreigners and people you don't know—or care to know. Geneviève and I had a meal there last month which was frankly disappointing. They of course apologized and refused to let us pay, but we wished we had stayed at home to enjoy Mme Constant's lobster bisque with oranges and her braised tongue." Turning to Mme Grabois, Michel sought confirmation, and attempted to include her in the conversation, to little avail however, as the poor woman had lost most of her hearing, and contributed to the conversation only by smiling and nodding occasionally.

Claudine mentioned that she and Olivier had dined at the Grand Véfour the week before with a young attorney and his wife. "The meal was delightful even though the company was not exactly to my taste." Michel asked her playfully, "You don't like young lawyers?" to which Claudine responded, "It's rather that I mistrust their pretty, flirtatious wives."

Michel, attracted by another of his favorite topics, asked "You certainly don't mind a little flirting, do you?" and Claudine smilingly rejoined, "As long as it's in good taste."

"I know no other kind."

"Olivier does."

Olivier had been listening with a smile on his face until this last not-so-playful jab: "You're not suggesting, my dear, that I was flirting with young Mme Tardieu?"

"Let's just say that at times you seemed less interested in your breast of veal than in..."

"That's enough, Claudine."

Not enough for deGrael, however, who warmed to the subject, "You know, Claudine, there's only one way to deal with a wayward husband."

"What's that, Michel?"

"Be a wayward wife."

Geneviève cleared her throat in a mockingly dramatic tone, and changed the subject, asking pleasantly, "What are your vacation plans this summer, Olivier?"

"We'll spend most of the month in Burgundy, with a few days on the Riviera visiting our children."

"Why don't you plan to spend a few days with us in St.-Tropez? We'll be there all of August, and probably bored to tears with the usual acquaintances to call on." Geneviève dutifully tried again to include her mother in the conversation, "Frightfully boring our Augusts in St.-Tropez, aren't they, Mother?" and got a cheerful smile in response.

At this point a liveried servant opened the door to the adjoining dining room set elegantly for five, and Geneviève invited the two guests to precede them and to take seats on opposite sides of the table. She then sat next to Olivier while Michel ceremoniously held Claudine's chair for her before seating Mme Grabois at the head of the table and then sat himself next to Claudine. They sipped champagne, dined on truffled foie gras, pheasant and delicate pastries, passed in review the political, social and economic events of the week, and laughed increasingly as the good food, good wine and verbal charm enveloped them in mirthful warmth. The dinner proceeded with a slow and seductive elegance which paralleled the elegant seductiveness of the conversation, ranging from vacations to gastronomy, from sport to fashion, from theatre to politics, all with a delicately polite flirtatious undertone.

Towards the close of the meal, while Geneviève deGrael, her mother, Mme Grabois, and Claudine were energetically dissecting a bit of gossip surrounding the wife of the President of the Republic, Michel, practically unnoticed by all, passed around the table behind Olivier, gently took his arm, and escorted him into the living room where he poured two generous glasses of cognac from a hundred-year-old bottle of Hennessy, opened a silver cigar box, and invited him to enjoy one of his Havanas.

"While the women are dawdling over their champagne and dessert, I wanted to take a few minutes to talk business with you, Olivier."

"Certainly, Michel."

"You've undoubtedly read of the shake-up in my Ministry. I've asked for the resignations of three of my Ministry Secretaries: Jarvais, Denis and Varlet. An accumulation of personal and political differences had made it impossible for me to continue working with them; they had in fact sought to oust me from my position."

"How outrageously ungrateful of them!"

"Yes, it is true that I raised the three of them from absolute obscurity. But that is often the way in politics. It has been a bitter struggle, but with the support of the Prime Minister, I have survived the crisis."

"And justice has been served!"

"It is my intent to name you, Olivier, to a high position in my Ministry, at least at the Secretary level. This too will be a bit of a struggle. As you know, many old-timers in the Interior Ministry have no confidence in the judiciary. We are a very politically sensitive organism of the government and the 'impartiality' of the magistrature is often perceived as disloyalty."

"I am aware of these prejudices, and am very grateful for your confidence in me."

"Fortunately, the record of your career is brilliant. To those who might want to accuse me of appointing a personal acquaintance unqualified to assume the responsibilities of a Ministry Secretary, I can cite many highly favorable newspaper accounts of decisions you have rendered. Your knowledge of the law is legendary. And perhaps most importantly, your character is beyond reproach. Yet, we must proceed slowly and avoid outright conflict—there has already been too much of that, and too much bad publicity stemming from it. I think it will be useful for you to meet socially some of the stalwarts of the Ministry; I'd like to invite you and Claudine to accompany me Saturday to a reception at the home of M. de Gennevilliers; many of Interior's highest officials will be there. It will be good for them to see you with me. Can you come?"

"My wife had planned to have us spend the weekend in Burgundy, but I believe the plans can be changed. Yes, certainly, Michel…"

Interrupted by voices, laughter and the opening of the living-room door, Michel and Olivier turned good-naturedly and with some actual relief to the invasion of the too-long abandoned women. Claudine led the way boldly, "So, you thought you could escape our civilizing influence by sneaking into the living room? And I bet you're discussing high affairs of state and other rubbish."

Fearing that Claudine had perhaps sipped a bit too much champagne and was in danger of creating a scene, Olivier tried to alert her with a fierce stare which contrasted with the gentleness of his voice, "We merely thought to spare you our cigar fumes, Claudine. You are certainly welcome to civilize us."

"I hold out little hope for you, Olivier, but Michel, as I am delighted to observe, still seems eminently civilizable."

"I'm sure my wife would disagree. But you've always brought out the best in me, Claudine."

"You see what I mean; he's perfectly gallant. Don't you think so, Mme Grabois."

"Excuse me, my dear?"

A word about Mme Grabois: Geneviève's mother had long been a bit of a social problem. She was dull-witted to begin with, and the years of her winding life had robbed her of not only a good deal of her sight and hearing. She lived alone and took her meals with her daughter and son-in-law. Usually only dimly aware of her surroundings, she took little notice of them, and they took even less notice of her. "A bump on a log," or a "flower on the wall," serve as appropriate images. Geneviève and Michel tolerated and ignored her. Occasionally a well-intentioned guest would politely try to include her in conversation and suffer the consequences. Claudine persisted, "Don't you agree that Michel is delightful company?"

"No, dear, he doesn't work for the light company; he's a minister of some kind."

There was a gradual shift to the sofas, as the ladies sipped on Grand Marnier while the men continued with their cognac. Claudine and Michel were paired together on one; Olivier and Geneviève were on another. Mme Grabois was between the two sofas, lost in both conversations.

Predictably they talked about food, restaurants and vacations. Geneviève remembered her unanswered invitation from earlier in the evening "Why don't you plan to spend a few days with us in St.-Tropez?" Michel chimed in, "Excellent idea! Can we count on it, Olivier?"

"Well, certainly; I'm sure Claudine and I would be delighted. As you know, our daughter Nicole and her family live in Antibes, and we usually spend some time there and in Monaco with Claudine's cousin. We could certainly fit in a few days in St.-Tropez."

"Wonderful! Your presence might even inspire Geneviève to do a little sailing. It's been three years since she has set foot on our yacht."

As Geneviève acquiesced, Michel remembered that his invitation for the following Saturday night had not yet been conveyed to Claudine, "Oh, and Geneviève, I've invited Claudine and Olivier to accompany us Saturday night to the reception at the Genevilliers'. It will probably be very dull, but there are some people Olivier should meet. We won't stay long. You would like to come, wouldn't you, Claudine?"

"Well, yes, of course. As it turns out, our other plans for the weekend seem to have fallen through."

"Good, we'll pick you up around 9:30."

The name Genevilliers stirred Claudine's memory, "Tell me, Michel, didn't I read something about the Genevilliers in the paper recently."

"Yes, there was an article about Juliette's fabulous Fabergé Easter Egg collection which she had loaned to the Children's Relief Society for a fund-raising exhibit. In two days, more than eight thousand people from all over France toured the exhibit which raised nearly four hundred thousand francs for the Society. There were detailed descriptions of most of the pieces, some of which had never been exhibited and which today are worth millions of francs."

Her curiosity strangely aroused and wishing to hear more about priceless Easter eggs and other antique treasures, Claudine sought to prolong the conversation, "I certainly would not feel comfortable having such valuable objects in my home."

Geneviève explained that Juliette Genevilliers seemed quite uncon-
cerned. "They are on open display in her reception rooms. One wanders
around their home eating canapés and cookies, dropping crumbs on
seventeenth century artworks and antiques. It's quite impressive. As you
can see, we have a few valuable pieces which have been in my family for
years but nothing like what one finds in the Genevilliers' home." Geneviève pointed to a corner of the living room with a Restoration *chaise
longue* and a set of mahogany shelves adorned with old volumes, porcelain figures and a miniature oil painting. Olivier looked at his watch dis-
creetly and with a look to Claudine confirmed that they could politely
take leave, "Well, I suppose we should be going. This has been a delightful evening, Michel and Geneviève."

Claudine concurred. "It certainly has been, and we thank you for
inviting us."

Geneviève tried politely to retain them longer, "Must you really leave
so early? It's only 11 o'clock."

"You know what the life of a working man is like, Geneviève. I have
an important staff meeting at 9 tomorrow and several files to review
before then."

Claudine took advantage of the opportunity to corroborate Olivier's
anti-social work habits, "I assure you, Geneviève, that Olivier has
become a real bore; he works all the time, gets up early in the morning
to read and write, and is rarely home in the evening before 8. And even
on weekends, I can't get him to leave his work behind."

Olivier chimed in at this point, "I am sure you understand that we
would like to stay longer; your company, as always, has been delightful. I
thank you for a wonderful meal and evening."

As Geneviève went out into the hallway to find the d'Anglades' coats,
and while Michel was preoccupied trying to explain to Mme Grabois
that the d'Anglades were leaving and that she would do well do say good
night to them, a remarkable scene took place in the corner of the living
room to which Geneviève had earlier referred. Olivier, who had indis-
cernibly edged his way back towards the mahogany shelves, in full view
of his wife, removed from one of the shelves a Sèvres porcelain figurine

of Joan of Arc and slipped it into his pocket. Claudine's eyes widened in amazement, but it happened so quickly that she wasn't sure what she had seen. She moved to him and placed her hand on his shoulder, as Olivier smilingly wished Mme Grabois a good night.

Geneviève entered with their coats, and she and Michel helped them with them. Olivier and Claudine, with additional profusions of thanks and reminders from the deGraels about Saturday night made their way out the door, leaving Michel and Geneviève satisfied with their evening and Michel more convinced than ever that even the most conservative members of his ministry staff would have to admit that Olivier was a man of the greatest tact, diplomacy, and integrity.

Without a word or even a glance at one another, Olivier and Claudine climbed into the back seat of the large ministry car waiting for them in front of the deGrael's apartment building. Both could think of nothing but the porcelain statue which bulged slightly from Olivier's right pants pocket; but really they could not think about the statue either. It was too unlikely, too impossible; even though both willed the theft and partici-pated in it.

Claudine, sitting to the right of Olivier on the plush leather seat, looked down towards Olivier's leg, reached out her hand to touch and caress the figurine, and then slid her hand a little farther and found, as she expected, that Olivier was nearly as erect and hard as the statue.

As the car wound its way around the Place de la Madeleine, the Place de la Concorde, crossed the Seine, passed in front of the *Chambre des Députés*, and took the rue de Bourgogne to the rue de Varenne, Clau-dine and Olivier, without attracting the notice of their ministry chauf-feur, engaged in discreet and nearly silent sexual activity, which left them, as the car turned into the rue de Jouy, wet and limp but by no means satisfied. All the chauffeur observed was a marked eagerness to escape from his car, a quick but still polite and cordial thank you, and their hurried retreat into the darkness of their apartment building.

CHAPTER 4

The next morning around 10:30 in the Friedland Gallery, littered with the debris from the previous night's opening, Joanne was serving a breakfast of café au lait and croissants on a table set up in the midst of the exhibit. As she offered Jacques a large bowl of coffee, he asked solicitously, "Are you sure you feel all right?"

"Sure, just a little groggy."

"Too much champagne?"

"Someone had to drink it."

"Yeah, sure."

Joanne sat down and as she buttered her croissant muttered, "Well, we win some and we lose some."

Jacques looked up and asked rhetorically, "Have we ever had a worse opening?"

Joanne winced, "No. Not even close. I don't think we had twenty-five people all night, and only one or two were real customers. Mainly our friends and their friends and a couple of students."

Jacques looked around at the messy debris and observed, "We still managed to drink twenty bottles of champagne."

Joanne groaned with her hand to her head: "I took care of most of that myself."

Jacques softly gave vent to frustration, "The worst part was that nobody had anything nice to say about the exhibit, even Richard's friends."

Joanne tried to counter Jacques' slight overstatement, "Some of the comments could be interpreted positively."

"Like?"

"Well, like Frédéric Leblanc telling Richard that he found the feathers very much in the tradition of contemporary cinema."

"That was fine until he started referring to…"

"Frédéric was drunk."

"Fortunately we all were."

"Who was that young effeminate fellow who stood dreamily in front of "Romeo" for fifteen minutes without saying a word?"

"He's a student of Richard's, one of the few he still has left. I asked him what particularly appealed to him in that piece, and, well, he sort of sounded like Richard: 'In an indifferent world, only a true artist can feel and appreciate the true weight of things.'"

"Richard has taught him a lot."

Jacques reached for a second croissant and asked disconsolately, "In the course of the evening, did you hear anyone say anything intelligent about the exhibit?"

"Yes, one of the real customers said she didn't think her crowded house was an appropriate space for Richard's sculptures."

"You have to wonder just what is an appropriate space for Richard's sculpture."

Joanne looked at Jacques reproachfully, "Did you talk to Nicole Adriane while she was here?"

"Well, I listened to her for awhile."

"Did she have any insights?"

"She kept wondering aloud why Richard didn't use fur instead of feathers."

"Which of course irritated the animal lovers. And Richard who thought that she as an artist and friend ought to appreciate his struggle to make bronze soar, as he put it."

Jacques and Joanne continued in their vain efforts to remember and to put a positive spin on bits of conversation from the previous evening. Jacques remembered a discussion about the priority of aesthetics versus philosophy in the conception of a work of art which had gotten pretty heated. Joanne commented that it was strange to see artists, mild, gentle creatures that they normally are, get so angry and vindictive, at which point Jacques remembered one of the most uncomfortable moments of the evening when Richard and one of his artist friends had found a common ground of agreement, the lack of taste among the contemporary public, which of course offended the few faithful customers who had bothered to show up.

At that moment the door opened and Richard entered with Martine, both looking pretty glum. Richard had the newspaper. They exchanged ritual kisses and greetings, and in response to Joanne's hesitant, "And how do you two feel this morning?" Richard responded with a wan smile, "Not as well as could be expected. We really flopped, didn't we?"

Joanne responded warmly to Richard's charm, "Yes, but we had a good time flopping."

"Speak for yourself."

"Well, for a man whose exhibit was flopping all around us, you really appeared to be having a good time."

Abandoning his candor and charm, Richard assumed one of his too well known attitudes and responded theatrically, "It should have been obvious to you, my true friends and protectors, that my gayety was false, that my heart was really breaking. So few there to admire my work! And so little comprehension from my fellow artists!"

Jacques motioned impatiently to the paper, "And what does friend Raymond have to say?"

Continuing his theatrical pose, Richard picked up the paper, "This you'll have to hear to believe: 'Jacques and Joanne Friedland, whose gallery on the rue de Seine has for many years been the herald of new artists and new movements, have gone out on a limb this week, have gone out on a rather precarious limb with Richard Rosendale and twenty of his 'Feathered Friends'. Will the bough break? We don't think so. Rosendale's feathered sculptures seem light enough, and besides no one is likely to rock the cradle. Certainly not this critic who enjoyed the airy presentation of some genuinely original pieces.'"

As Richard looked up, Joanne exclaimed, "Not bad!"

"Not particularly good either; I think he should have been more descriptive. After reading that you really wouldn't know what to expect. He makes it sound like a wildlife exhibit, and not a very interesting one at that."

Jacques found encouragement in the brief notice, "He said nothing negative and at least two positives."

"Two positives?"

"Genuinely original and light."

"One positive and one semi-positive."

Joanne agreed with Jacques that Raymond had tried to be helpful. "That's all you can really hope for in this business, Richard. Raymond is not the problem. His critique can't harm or help an exhibit that no one was curious enough to come to see."

"Touché! Maybe it was just a bad night, lots of other things going on."

"Richard, we carefully selected Wednesday, April 11, as a perfect night for an opening. At least give us credit for knowing that much about our business."

"And how many invitations did you send out?"

"Two thousand."

"And only about twenty people bothered to show up. For good free champagne—and me!"

"That's about it."

"And most of the guests forgot why they were here; my poor 'Feathered Friends' were neglected by the guests."

"Not by all of them," Joanne reminded him. "There was Christine Landais who decided that Orion looked like he needed a drink and proceeded to pour half a bottle of champagne into him before we could stop her."

Richard chuckled. "Christine was just having a good time, I suppose. It didn't hurt Orion at all. And Roland Davaut was in rare form too. I don't think I've ever seen him that drunk. We had to physically restrain him from removing his clothes and adorning himself with feathers. He wanted to be a feathered friend and exhibit himself in the loft."

"You should be flattered. We also committed a sacrilege against the operatic arts. I'm surprised that our rendition of the Toreador song didn't have the riot police down on us. What inspired that anyway?"

Jacques chimed in, "It was when Roland noticed that Pyro resembles an erect bull."

"Oh yes, of course. Another flattering tribute to my work. And what do we do now?"

Joanne looked at Jacques, who answered gently, "I am afraid Richard that we have to start thinking about our next exhibit."

"You're going to close me down?"

Joanne reminded Richard that they had a contract for a week. "We'll carry the exhibit an extra couple of days through next weekend. But it won't do you or us any good to leave this up and have no one come by to see it."

"Don't you want to starve with us? There can be solidarity in starvation, Joanne. And aren't you jumping to conclusions? Just because no one showed last night…"

Joanne looked at her watch. "The gallery has been open for an hour already this morning; people have had time to read this morning's paper. No one is here, Richard."

"Well, where are they?"

Jacques looked out the front window, down the rue de Seine, and reported, "The good citizens of Paris, whether they be art lovers or not, are going calmly about their business this morning, not at all conscious that last night was a personal disaster for you and a commercial failure for us."

"Disaster? Failure? Hey, it's just an exhibit. I have succeeded, I have created twenty sculptures which will live forever! You have demonstrated great wisdom and perceptiveness by inviting me to exhibit them here. Art history will record the name of the Friedland Gallery, and the names of its brilliant owners, who recognized the genius of Rosendale's feathered sculptures and first tried to show them to an uncomprehending public. In my museum there will undoubtedly be a plaque describing your efforts on my behalf and extolling your brilliant judgment. You like me are way ahead of your time. Why do you realize that ten years after Einstein published his theory of relativity, there were still only three people in the world who could yet understand it? Now we predict that within another decade, every physics student in the world will understand and appreciate its brilliance and beauty. So let it be with me."

Joanne put her arm around Richard's shoulder. "There's plenty more coffee and croissants, Richard and Martine. Have a seat. Do us the honor of letting us have breakfast with the sculptor Richard Rosendale whose 'Feathered Friends' will forever testify to our friendship, if not to our commercial judgment."

Richard smiled, "I really did have a good time last night. Despite the 'failure' of the exhibit, the presence of friends like you—and even some of the others—plus your excellent champagne, well, it was a great party."

Joanne remained worried about Richard's shaky morale, "Let me ask you your own question. What are you going to do now?"

"I'll be back in my studio this afternoon, as soon as I recover from this hangover."

"More 'feathered friends'?"

"Maybe. But I think I'll do a little less thinking and a little more creating. When you come right down to it, this stuff is pretty cerebral. I might have gone off on the wrong track trying to conceptualize these statues before creating them. Last night Nicole and I argued about the priority of aesthetics and philosophy in art. She may be right: what a work looks like is more important than what it means. I'm maybe too hung up on meaning—at least for contemporary Paris. And I have plans to get together with Raymond; we agreed last night that we haven't seen enough of one another recently. He may have some useful suggestions for my future work."

Joanne found Richard's words encouraging, "Sounds like you're thinking a little more commercially."

"Despite appearances, I really have nothing against eating. There's no reason why I can't create for tomorrow and at the same time eat today."

"I don't know if that's wisdom or cop-out."
"I don't either. I'll have to think that through."

CHAPTER 5

That same morning, in the apartment on the rue Barbet de Jouy, M. and Mme Brunot were curiously disoriented, as at 10:45, both the baron and baroness were still asleep.

M. Brunot was seated at the kitchen table, unsure what to do next, as his wife entered, exclaiming, "It's almost eleven o'clock, and they're both still asleep!"

"When I tried to arouse the Baron at 7:30, he told me quite rudely to let him be. Even when I reminded him of his 9 o'clock meeting."

"They must have been out late last night."

"Very unlike the Baron."

A sound of slippered footsteps in the hallway alerted them that one of their masters was approaching. It was Claudine, sleepily radiant, barely concealing her arrogant amusement at the servants' dismay.

"Good morning, madame. I'll get your breakfast."

"Thank you, Mme Brunot." As she wandered into the dining room, Claudine noticed that Olivier's coat was hung by the door, and called back to M. Brunot, with an air of amused surprise, "My husband isn't up yet?"

"No, madame. I tried to arouse him at 7:30, but he refused to get up. I called the Courthouse at 8 and told them the Baron was ill and probably wouldn't be able to appear this morning."

"You did well, thank you." As M. Brunot exited, Claudine went to the phone and dialed her hairdresser. "Hello, Victor, this is Mme d'Anglade.

Say, I'm awfully sorry I missed my appointment this morning…Well, that's very gracious of you, but I certainly should have called you sooner…Oh, no, I'm really all right, just a little under the weather this morning and thought I should stay in. I'm much better now. Do you think you could fit me in this afternoon?…That will suit me just fine; I'll be there at 4. Well, thank you." She hung up and stared dreamily into space for a few minutes, her thoughts impenetrably private. After a while, Olivier entered sleepily. He and Claudine stared at each other and then burst out laughing. Finally, it was Claudine who asked the obvious, "My God! All night long! What is going on?"

"I don't really know. All sorts of metaphors come to mind."

"Like what?"

"Like a champagne bottle blowing its cork."

"Repeatedly?"

"Why not? Or a pressure cooker?"

"After years of pressure building up."

"Or a volcanic eruption."

"On a deserted island."

"Or a monk on sabbatical leave…"

"With a nun."

"I didn't really know what was happening as we ran out of deGrael's apartment…"

"But you had guessed by the time we got home."

"Do you suppose the driver could see what we were doing?"

"It would have been hard for him not to."

Amidst their giggles, Mme Brunot entered with breakfast for Claudine. There was an embarrassed silence as she served. "I will bring the Baron's breakfast immediately. Will the Baron be needing my husband this morning?"

"No, I won't be going to work until after lunch."

"Very well, I'll tell him that."

Olivier and Claudine renewed their giggling, which was briefly interrupted by Olivier's sobering thought, "What do you suppose my colleagues will think of my absence?"

"Brunot took care of it; he phoned in to say that you're ill."

"The first staff meeting I've missed in three years!"

"Even the best legal mind in all of France can occasionally have a fever."

"I suppose so." And then with an air of half-felt mistrust, "Where in the world did you learn all that?"

"All what?"

"All those things we did last night."

"Do you really want to know all the places in the world where I learned all that?"

"Perhaps not. But what happened? Why all of a sudden after years of once-a-week dutiful intercourse, did we suddenly—it certainly was sudden—come to spend a whole night repeatedly making love in every imaginable position…"

"Not quite <u>every</u> imaginable position…"

"…until we finally fell asleep from exhaustion at 6 A.M."

"It was obviously because of the statue."

"The statue?"

"Yes, the Sèvres figurine of Joan of Arc which you stole from the deGrael's living room."

"You know, I had almost forgotten about that."

"Whatever led you to take it anyway? I have to admit that at first I couldn't believe my eyes."

"I actually stole a valuable eighteenth century porcelain figurine from the home of my friend and benefactor Michel deGrael! I can't believe it either."

"Why did you?"

"I'm not sure. I remember we were talking about the Genevilliers' Fabergé collection. You and Geneviève mentioned the possibility of those items being stolen, and suddenly the idea of stealing a valuable antique appeared to me—through the glow of the champagne and cognac I had drunk—as a fascinating, exciting—yes, sexually exciting—adventure. I then noticed the Sèvres figurines which Geneviève had casually pointed to, and felt a swell of emotion, adrenaline to the heart, blood to the genitals, which left me weak and breathless. When, for just a few seconds, I felt I was unobserved, I rushed to the statue of Joan of Arc and grabbed it. I chose the statue of Joan because of its size, but also because the thought that my victim was a virgin, a saint and a martyr, well, it added to the excitement."

"It's strange, but I felt the same sort of excitement at Geneviève's description of the Genevilliers' home, and the idea of theft occurred to me as a wildly delicious temptation, and then I noticed the look in your eye and your excitement. It quite took my breath away too, and then when I saw you take the figurine, it just overwhelmed me. There you were, fulfilling my fantasy, in a state of sexual excitement. You were irresistible, Olivier!"

"What a strange phenomenon! And what a strange couple we have turned out to be! After twenty-six years of marital orthodoxy."

"Who would have thought that the ever so respectable Baron Olivier d'Anglade, President of the Paris Court of Appeals, and his ever so fashionable and elegant wife Claudine would turn out to be a pair of thieves and sexual perverts."

"Please, Claudine, don't get carried away. One statue does not a thief make, nor one night of pleasure a pervert."

"We can't stop now, Olivier."

"We can't?"

"Didn't last night mean anything to you?"

"Of course it did! I've never been so aroused, so happy, so alive in all my life."

"That's exactly the way I feel."

"But we can't let the search for pleasure become the purpose and goal of our lives."

"Why not?"

"Because we are civilized human beings, endowed with reason and dignity."

At this point, Mme Brunot brought in the baron's breakfast. Olivier reviewed in his mind their last few remarks and concluded that it was quite possible that Mme Brunot had overheard much of their conversation and chosen this moment to interrupt them. Her face of course showed nothing, and never would. But he vowed to himself to be more prudent.

"Would you like anything else, sir?"

"No, that's perfect, Mme Brunot." She exited with a completely blank expression. Claudine sensed her husband's concern and continued in a lowered voice, "For fifty-two years, Olivier, you have been a boring human being, endowed with repressive guilt and stultifying cowardice. You have been dead for the first fifty-two years of your life. You yourself just said that you have never before felt so aroused, so happy, so alive in all your life as you did last night. Now that you have tasted life, can you return to the dead?"

"But isn't my ambition, my desire for power and glory part of life too? I am confident that my reason and dignity will be rewarded, that if I continue as I have, Michel will name me undersecretary and that my career will take off from there. Last night after dinner, while you ladies were still at the table, Michel told me in no uncertain terms that he intends to name me to his cabinet. Can you ask me to give that up?"

"I'm not asking you to give up your ambition, just your guilt and cowardice."

"Can an undersecretary be a thief?"

"Of course he can; it happens all the time. Besides, you will never be suspected of theft, Olivier. Geneviève and Michel will eventually notice that their Sèvres Joan of Arc is missing. But even if in their reasoning on its absence they conclude that it must have disappeared at the moment when Geneviève was getting our coats and when Michel was dealing with his mother-in-law, they would never in a million years let the possibility cross their minds that the ever so respectful Baron d'Anglade or his elegant wife had anything to do with its disappearance. They would first of all suspect their servants, a sneak thief, or even one another, before they would think of us."

"It is true that those were my very thoughts as I was tempted to steal the statue."

"Even after a thousand similar thefts, the victims will invent all sorts of illogical solutions rather than suspect either of us."

"I am sure that you are right."

"So, on Saturday, which of us will take a Fabergé Easter Egg from the Genevilliers' home?"

"What?"

"Well, isn't that the logical next step?"

"It's insane!"

"It's life! And you will be amply rewarded."

"I'm sure of that." After a moment's reflection, Olivier went on, "Michel invited us on Saturday night so that his colleagues in the Interior Ministry will have a favorable impression of me. So, I will show them what a clever thief I can be."

"You'll not show them that at all. You'll dazzle them with your wit, tact and diplomacy, while committing the perfect crime."

"Claudine, in twenty years as a jurist, I have met hundreds of brilliant and ambitious people who committed the perfect crime. Most of them are still in jail."

"Yes, but none of them had your knowledge of criminal behavior, your fine legal mind, your spotless reputation—and your total lack of any apparent motive for theft."

"That is a real protection. Who would suspect a generous, wealthy man, with no known passion for art objects, of scheming to steal them? What possible reason could I, Olivier d'Anglade, have for stealing art treasures? The apparent gratuitousness of the crime is not only a protection, it's an incentive."

Claudine, feigned pique, "An incentive?"

"Not that I need any additional incentives, my dear."

"I should hope not."

"Most criminal investigations rely on obvious motives, who would most benefit from the criminal act. Following the theft of an art object, the police look for a man in need of money, or a connoisseur. I am neither. No one would guess my real motive…"

"Oh really?"

"It will be a pleasure to match wits with the police and confound them, an ironic consolation for the scorn in which the police tradition-ally hold the magistrature, a vengeance for the obstacle they represent for my ambition. I am also deeply intrigued with the psychological ram-ifications…"

"Do you mean the sexual ramifications?"

"Well, yes I do."

"So, you'll do it for me, on Saturday night!"

"But how can we do it? A Fabergé Easter Egg will not fit as easily into my pocket as a small figurine. There will be crowds of people in every reception room. People will be paying close attention to me—and to you, as the rumor is already circulating that I am to be the new underse-cretary. With all these people, under all this scrutiny, how can I possibly steal a large cumbersome object, carry it out of the house and bring it home in the Minister's car!"

"This will be a challenge. You know, Olivier, just the thought of it, well, I find this very exciting…"

It was curious to both Olivier and Claudine that they found in the deGraels' evocation of the Genevillier's Fabergé egg collection a source of sexual excitement. While they had always had a keen interest in the fine arts and collected a few interesting paintings and porcelains, they had rarely discussed their interest in art, and collecting was never a pas-sion for them. Claudine smiled as she suddenly recollected, "You know, Olivier, I have had premonitions of this sort of thing. Certain works of art have fascinated me, and, while not realizing that the attraction was sexual, I have often myself staring fixedly at them, and desiring to pos-sess them."

Olivier went to the courthouse that afternoon, tired and distracted enough to lend easy credence to the story of his indisposition. Claudine dutifully visited her hairdresser, but had little interest in Victor's witty chatter. By six that evening they were sequestered in Claudine's dressing room, discussing in hushed tones Saturday night's plan of action. Clau-dine would sew into her petticoat a large pouch, suspended from the front and back of the top, so that the pouch, when filled with the Fabergé, egg would hang between her legs just above the knees. While Olivier supervised and admired his wife's dexterity, she created the pouch from a pair of her finest silk bloomers. As she worked, they joked rather stupidly about lifting her dress and inserting and removing the egg from the pouch.

After dinner, she practiced for several hours walking naturally, with a weighted box in the pouch, until both were satisfied that no one observing her would find anything strange in her demeanor. Concerned that getting in and out of the deGrael's car on the way home might be awkward, they agreed to call in the morning, advising them that they would take a cab home from the Genevilliers' so that they would be free to leave early. While seated in the back of the cab, they would transfer the egg from her pouch to a plain paper sack which Olivier would keep folded in his breast pocket.

Olivier and Claudine spent most of Saturday secluded in their rooms, resting, reading, working a little, and going over in their minds the strange turn that their lives had taken. They were ready by 9 P.M. and waited nervously for thirty minutes the arrival of the deGrael's ministry car. From the rue de Jouy to the Genevilliers' apartment on the rue Auber, the intensity of their chatter amused Michel deGrael who naively attributed their emotion to the political importance of the gathering.

By the time Olivier and Claudine arrived with the deGraels at the Genevilliers', there were crowds of people at the reception, and all seemed eager to have a chance to observe, listen to and chat with the renowned jurist and his elegant wife. Rumors of his impending appointment enhanced the curiosity and whetted the interest of well-wishers as well as those who resented his reputation and good fortune. Olivier and Claudine actually seemed to attract more attention than the deGraels, which was somewhat disconcerting for all four.

It was in 1931 during a visit to Berlin that the Marquis de Genevilliers began his Fabergé collection. Within three years, he had acquired twelve of the jeweled masterpieces which were exhibited publicly in March of 1936 in their Paris apartment. As Geneviève deGrael had noted, the eggs, along with many antique treasures acquired by the Genevilliers, adorned several of the salons in their spacious right bank apartment.

Peter Carl Fabergé was only twenty-four years old in 1870 when he took over the family jewelry business in St. Petersburg. He quickly assembled a group of artists and craftsmen who brought to the jewelry trade a revolutionary interest in craftsmanship. One of these craftsmen, Michael Evlampievich Perchin, joined the House of Fabergé in 1886, and at the age of twenty-six became the company's leading work master. It was he who created the first Imperial Easter Egg and who signed all of the eggs produced until 1903 when he left the firm. He was succeeded by Henrik Wigström. The first eggs produced by the House of Fabergé were for Czar Alexander III; his son Nicholas II continued the tradition, and in the years from 1886 to 1919, a total of fifty-three eggs were produced for the imperial family. Yet others were produced for wealthy families such as the Kelch family, the Nobel family and the Duchess of Marlborough. In the wake of the 1917 revolution, the Fabergé eggs produced for the imperial family were eventually authorized for sale by the Ministry of Foreign Trade and were dispersed from Berlin throughout Europe; some even traveled back and forth between Europe and America with the baggage of entrepreneurial collectors such as Armand Hammer, Lansdell K. Christie and Malcolm Forbes.

As the evening wore on, and people started to leave, Olivier and Claudine quite unexpectedly but quite naturally found themselves alone in a small reception room in which one of the Fabergé eggs was unpretentiously displayed on a table in a dimly lit corner. It was the Chanticleer Egg, a 1903 creation of Michael Perchin which Nicholas II presented to his mother, Maria Feodorovna. The egg is a clock which features a small golden rooster enameled in yellow, blue and green, its feathers set with diamonds, which emerges from the top to crow every hour. Its head, wings and beak move. The egg and the four panels of the base are enameled in a sapphire blue. Ribbons of gold encircle the top of the egg below the rooster. The white enamel clock face is adorned with gold and seed pearls. The panels of the pedestal bear gold armorial motifs symbolizing music and medicine (special interests of Maria Feodorovna). It is one of the largest of the imperial eggs; at 12 and 5/8 inches, only the Uspensky Cathedral Egg stands taller.

In seconds Olivier removed it from the table, inserted it into Claudine's pouch, and the two returned to a crowded room to converse gaily with other guests. The eventual leave-taking and the ride home in the pre-arranged taxi went as smoothly as could be hoped.

The night following this theft was more passionate than the night following the theft of the Joan of Arc statue. To Olivier's astonishment, Claudine was even more attentive, inventive, and abandoned in her love-making. She seemed to be rewarding him as well as responding to her own sensations. Her attentions were quite extraordinary, thrilling, unlike anything he had ever experienced from any of his mistresses. In the course of the night they created a perverse little system of wagers and rewards, designed to excite each other's thirst for further thefts by associating the degree of difficulty with specific sexual rewards. Absent from their conversation was any concern for the morality of their conduct or the dangers of discovery and disgrace. They formed the outline of a plan for a criminal campaign to carry them through the summer at the rate of one theft per week.

CHAPTER 6

Most Parisians didn't notice or gave little thought to a small *fait divers* which appeared in the April 17, 1936 edition of *France Soir*, announcing the apparent suicide drowning of a distraught American artist, Richard Rosendale. There were few details, but the brief notice did refer to the opening of the artist's latest exhibit at the Friedland Gallery. However, the following day, *France-Soir*'s headlines screamed out in bold type, "*La Mort d'un Artiste Désespéré*", and followed up with details about the life and unsuccessful career of the young American artist, speculating that the final straw in his long and lonely battle against the art establishment had been the failure of his opening at the Friedland Gallery just days before. There were unfortunate graphic details about the nearly unrecognizable condition of the body which had been discovered after three to four days by some fishermen. In the days that followed several tabloid newspapers picked up the story, embellished with testimonies from several established artists; there were also highly flattering comments by gallery owner Jacques Friedland. The tabloids made much of Raymond Crosatier's brief and unenthusiastic review of the opening which appeared in the *Figaro*, but efforts to interview him failed, as he was apparently out of town on vacation.

Three weeks later, a pale and still teary-eyed Martine Lenouet was sadly packing up hers and Richard's belongings in their tiny apartment on the rue des Saints-Pères. She answered a knock on the door, and greeted Jacques and Joanne Friedland with a forced smile.

"We thought we'd come by to see if there was anything we could do to help."

Martine went over to the rusty hotplate on the kitchenette counter to boil some water, "Oh, I have almost everything packed up."

Joanne brushed her aside and took over the coffee-making with a motherly concern. "What are you doing with Richard's stuff?"

"I'm not really sure; his family doesn't seem much interested in it."

"They weren't much interested in him. They didn't even show up for the funeral."

Martine grimaced. "No…I've packed up some of his finished pieces that were here. I'll take them with me to my parents' house in Sceaux. There's really not much else, some clothing that's not worth saving, and a few odds and ends that I'll keep as mementos. I thought I'd let you two take care of his materials and equipment."

Jacques seated himself on the sofa bed by the window, and suggested gently to Martine, "Why don't you leave the finished pieces with us too. People have been asking about his work; I think we can sell them. It's what Richard would have wanted. I guess you can consider yourself his heir; Richard would have wanted that too."

Martine shrugged, "Who could possibly guess what Richard would have wanted?"

Jacques nodded and smiled, "Yeah, we're still kind of in shock too."

Martine, feeling she was among caring friends, burst into tears, "I can't help thinking about the way he was that last morning, the morning after the opening. Sure, he was disappointed, we all were. But he seemed determined to continue, even cheerful. I wasn't worried about him. So why?"

"Why?"

"Why did he throw himself into the Seine? When he disappeared that evening, I thought of all kinds of possibilities, even that one. But I couldn't really make myself believe that he might have killed himself. I still don't believe it."

Joanne sat beside her on the sofa and put her arm around Martine, "I don't either, Martine."

"I thought I understood him."

"How long had you two known each other?"

"We met about two years ago. I was working at the Café Rembrandt and he was there a lot. He told me later he was there a lot because I was there a lot. After about three weeks of seeing me there every day, he finally got up the nerve to start a conversation with me. He asked what I thought of the surrealist sculptures at the Passy Gallery. I answered that I had never seen them. So that was our first date: a gallery talk by Richard. He went on for two hours. Then we went to his apartment and I spent the night. I moved in with him the next day."

"Why?"

"There was something about him that was so strange, so different and for that reason so wonderful. He was shy and awkward, and those are certainly qualities that you don't find often in Paris. And he seemed so intelligent, and so sincerely profound. Oh, I know that he used to like to launch into bombastic speeches, using pretentious language and ridiculous metaphors, but that was just his public performance that he used in order to hide his sensitivity and shyness. He was a remarkably complex person, and so changeable. But he was always kind and considerate, never selfish or really egotistical. I guess all that I learned later. What attracted me to him at first was his awkwardness, his sincerity and his intelligence."

Joanne drifted over to the stove to continue the coffee preparation. "Did you keep on working at the café, after you moved in with Richard?"

"For a little while, but then Richard convinced me I should go back to school. I had started at the university with the idea of becoming a lawyer, but I quit after three months. It had seemed boring and pointless. I started again last fall. Richard helped me a lot; he was a real morale booster. And of course my parents were delighted when I went back to school. They had stopped supporting me when I quit; that's why I was working in the café. Now my parents are supporting me again."

Jacques smiled softly, "What did they think of Richard?"

"They've hardly ever met. They think he's a good influence on me, but they really don't understand art—and artists."

"Who does? And my livelihood depends on them."

"My parents asked me if they should go to the funeral, and I told them not to. I knew they'd feel terribly out of place. And of course they hate the publicity surrounding Richard's suicide."

Joanne came back to the sofa bringing three demi-tasse cups of dark coffee. "What are you going to do now, Martine?"

"I'll spend the summer at my family's house in Sceaux. I'll probably live there and commute to school in the fall. I don't think I could stand to live in this apartment without Richard. I'll finish my degree next June."

Jacques, looking for a way to be helpful, asked eagerly, "Do you need any help getting your stuff out to Sceaux?"

"Thanks, Jacques, but my parents are picking me and my things up tomorrow morning."

"So, everything is all set."

"I guess so. Richard Rosendale kills himself. I rearrange my life a little, and everything is 'all set.' It seems so strange that the death of a man should have such little effect on the world."

Jacques cleared his throat and began awkwardly, "There is something else, Martine…"

"What?"

"When I said that people have been asking about Richard's work, well…, there's really a lot of interest."

Jacques' tone puzzled Martine. "What do you mean?"

Joanne explained, "There's a lot of interest in Richard's sculptures. Several people want to buy his works."

"Now?"

Joanne went on, "Exactly. It happens all the time. Richard's death attracted a lot more attention than his life ever did. His exhibit got five centimeters on the back page of the *Figaro*'s art section. His death was plastered all over *France-Soir* and several tabloids for five days."

Martine was astonished, "Really? I didn't see any of the papers. Those days were just so unreal. Dreamlike but not a nightmare, because I was never really terrified. Just empty and unreal. I'd wake up in the morning expecting to find Richard fixing coffee. Then I'd go out and look for him. During the days he was missing, I crisscrossed Paris on foot, calling on his friends, casually asking if they had seen Richard; they, undoubtedly pretending they didn't know anything was wrong, answering just as casually that no, they hadn't seen him, then going on to cafés or museums where he liked to hang out, looking around, asking more people. Five days in a sleepwalk looking for Richard and finding only an empty café, and an artificially casual, 'No, we haven't seen him,' and an empty apartment every night. But now, when I think about those five days, well, at least then I could be hopeful; and so I look back on those days and wish I could relive them and make them end differently."

As Martine broke into muffled sobs, and tried to apologize, Joanne again put her arm around her: "That's all right, Martine. It's good to cry."

Martine gently smiled through her tears and asked naively, "Did the papers really write about Richard?"

Jacques answered enthusiastically, "Sure. An artist disappears the day after his exhibit flops. Exciting news! For five days there's no sign of him. Interest starts to wane, then bang!, on the fifth day a body tentatively identified as Richard is pulled from the Seine. Several tabloids sold lots of editions based on that. Pictures of Richard, pictures of the 'Feathered Friends.' And lots of people coming by the gallery to look, and buy."

"How horribly ironic!"

"It happens that way a lot. Pick up the biography of almost any great artist: a poor miserable existence, then the artist dies and his works are worth more money than he ever dreamed of: Gauguin, Rousseau, Pissarro."

"Richard used to fantasize about that. Too bad he can't see it actually happen."

"Yes, he'd be having a ball."

This thought provoked another of Martine's recent obsessions: "If only it were a mistake. If only that weren't his body. You told the police you weren't 100 percent sure."

Jacques conceded with a shrug. "The body had been in the water five days. I wasn't even 100 percent sure it was human. Oh, I'm sorry. But it was really an awful sight. But he was Richard's size and had on Richard's clothes and had Richard's empty wallet…"

Joanne interrupted, "I thought it was funny that there was no money in his wallet at all. One paper made a big deal of that, suggesting that maybe he was robbed and murdered."

Martine smiled, "I assure you there's nothing at all strange about Richard's wallet being completely empty. It happened all the time."

Jacques went on, "At any rate, I was sure, and so were the police. And so were the people at the funeral."

Joanne tried to guide the conversation in a healthier direction, "Wasn't that strange? All those people we didn't know, all those people who never knew Richard, there at his funeral. Drawn by morbid curiosity. The three of us were the only ones there who really knew him. No one came to his exhibit, but hundreds came to his funeral."

Martine added with some bitterness, "Richard was right to despise the public."

Joanne raised a question that had been troubling her, "I was surprised that Raymond Crosatier wasn't at the funeral. Have you heard from him?"

"No, nothing."

Jacques mentioned that he tried to call him, but there was no answer at home, and his paper said he was on vacation. "He must know about Richard. They were going to get together that very evening. Do you think he feels guilty?"

Martine generously defended him, "I hope not. His article didn't really help a lot, but he was just doing his job."

Jacques persisted, "He should have been at the funeral."

It was Martine's turn to change the subject, "You know, I'm a little happier now that you've told me people want to buy Richard's sculptures."

Joanne agreed. "It makes us feel better too. And I don't mean because of the money."

"Of course not. If only…"

At that point an extraordinary event interrupted Martine's obsessive thought, in fact interrupted everything: her life, her despair, her future.

At that moment, the door to her apartment opened, and in walked Richard Rosendale, looking like a *clochard*.

"Hi! It wasn't me!"

CHAPTER 7

Martine looked at him, with an uncomprehending stare. She started to shriek, gasped and then fainted. Jacques, Joanne and Richard all rushed to her. Jacques administered a few sips of brandy. Her eyes fluttered, then seemed to focus on Richard's, as he helped her up into a chair. She gradually revived as Richard repeatedly tried to reassure her that he was not a hallucination or a ghost, begging her forgiveness for the anguish he had caused. Finally, Joanne calmed them all with her insistent, obvious and logical question, "All right, Richard, so who was it?"

Richard then went on to explain excitedly that it was unfortunately their friend Raymond Crosatier. Pressed by the others he offered a full narration of the unlikely sequence of events of the evening when he disappeared:

"That afternoon I went to see Raymond at his office, as we had agreed to go out and have a drink together. I especially wanted to assure him that I wasn't angry about his article. He was cleaning off his desk, getting ready to leave on vacation and suggested we could get together after work. So, about six o'clock we got together and went to the Calumette Café, which is near his office. I was really feeling pretty good despite everything. My confidence in my ability hadn't been shaken: why should it have been? It wasn't a problem of people disliking my exhibit; no one even bothered to go to it. I saw it more as a public relations problem. People weren't interested in my work; they didn't know they should be."

"Raymond and I were drinking pretty heavily, and we talked about ways of attracting attention to my work. Different stunts which people couldn't help noticing. At one point I told him about this movie I saw about an artist who can't sell anything, and he and his friend come up with a fake suicide to attract attention. I thought maybe we could do something like that, but Raymond thought it was too risky, and too corny, and he pointed out incidentally that we'd need a body to make it really convincing."

"Well, it was after midnight when we were walking home, pretty drunk, and something amazing happened."

"What's that, Richard?"

"Raymond died."

"Died?" from the other three corners of the table.

"Heart attack. Just like that. We had drunk an awful lot, and Raymond had gotten pretty excited during a few of our arguments. And I remember that once he told me he had some kind of a heart condition. At any rate, I tried to revive him, but there was no way."

Joanne suspiciously wondered, "How did you know he was dead?"

"I had seen it before. I don't know if you remember my old friend Jean Belfourt, who was a medical student…Well, I had spent a lot of time with him, going his rounds, and got a pretty good medical education from it. There was no question in my mind that Raymond had suffered a massive heart attack and was very dead. I was drunk, and the movie came back to me. Now I had a body I could disguise as mine. We were about the same size; I knew a few days under water would disfigure him. So I switched clothes with him, leaving my wallet in his pocket after taking out the little money I had left. I weighted him down with anything I could find; rocks, bottles, which I stuffed into his clothes, and tossed him in."

The explanation left them all very uneasy; Jacques articulated the growing anxiety, "How could you possibly have hoped it would work? People are going to eventually miss Raymond."

"Remember I was very drunk. Everything seemed so easy to me. After it was all done, I fell asleep under a bridge, with a few other drunks, confident that my fortune was made. The next morning I woke up feeling awful: effects of the wine, depression about the gallery opening, but worst of all pure panic about what I had done to Raymond. It hit me in a flash that when they discovered Raymond's body, disguised in my clothing, the police would immediately assume I had killed him. Especially when they read the article Raymond had written about me, and then talked to people who had seen us together all evening. We had attracted a lot of attention in our drunkenness, and even shouted at one another in public a couple of times. It could really look bad for me."

"So, for three weeks I have been hiding out, living with the other street bums of Paris, begging for coins, sleeping under bridges, avoiding people for fear I might be recognized. I read the papers daily, read all the articles about me, even read about my funeral."

Martine burst into tears, "You weren't very considerate of us, Richard."

"Oh, Martine, I am sorry. I know you must have suffered at the thought I was dead. But just think how much I was suffering, and how scared I was. I just didn't know what to do. It kept amazing me that there was no word about Raymond. He had become quite a loner, but I was still surprised that no one reported him missing. I called his paper, and they told me he had just left on a two week vacation. So they hadn't missed him yet. I began to think that maybe I had gotten away with it, and decided to come tell Martine what I had done."

Joanne, who had grown increasingly annoyed, asked, "You didn't think you should call some of your old friends sooner?"

"Oh, Joanne, I was so confused and terrified, and ashamed. I thought you'd be outraged and turn me in."

"You're right about the outrage. Letting the three of us think you were dead for three weeks, people who really care about you, well…"

"So, you are furious at me?"

Martine looked at him with tears welling, "Richard, we're in shock. But really, for two weeks I've been waiting for you to show up. How can I be furious? I'm ecstatic! How have you lived for the past three weeks?"

"It's been a real education! I've been associating with lots of other non-people. It's amazing that once you put on a tattered, discarded raincoat, let your beard go for a few days, and stop combing your hair, you stop existing. People go past you without looking. If you hold out your hand, they sometimes give you money, but they don't look at you. If they look at you, they're affirming your existence, and they can't do that."

As Martine, Jacques and Joanne became increasingly used to the idea that Richard was indeed alive, the conversation became less urgent; they became more curious, intrigued, intellectually engaged in the adventure. Martine asked, "What did you live on, Richard?"

"Mostly bread and milk. A lot of grocery store clerks were surprised to have a bum come in to buy a liter of milk. I had no trouble collecting enough money for bread and milk, and I don't think I lost any weight."

"You mean you begged?" Martine asked with some disbelief.

"Why not? It's not much different from being an artist. I can't help comparing my social position with that of the artist in the Renaissance, when kings, princes, and members of the aristocracy tried to outbid one another to patronize the great artists of their time. Artists were invited to live in palaces and chateaux, fed, courted, admired and handsomely paid. Now, while the modern day equivalents of kings, princes and members of the aristocracy pay lip service to the arts, they all have horrible taste and are much too preoccupied with less durable forms of grandeur to bother even thinking about the starving artist. So we beg: we beg galleries to exhibit our works; we beg journalists to write about our exhibits; we beg the public to come see our works. We stop just short of begging them to buy, but the silent begging of our imploring eyes is not so far removed from the outstretched hand of my street brethren. I didn't really feel so out of place amongst them."

"You were able to communicate with the bums?"

"To some extent, but our differences in drinking habits was a bit of an obstacle."

"What are they like?"

"You know, they really don't exist. Those that drink all the time. They're in a state of perpetual absence. They don't understand anything beyond their present physical needs. Some of them are different; some remember the past, when they still existed, but it's usually either painful for them or obscure."

Jacques objected to the overwhelmingly negative image, "People say they're happy."

"They're not unhappy. Is that the same thing? If happiness is the absence of the consciousness of pain, then they're happy."

Richard suddenly realized that despite his earlier pronouncement about the adequacy of his milk and bread diet, he was very hungry. Within minutes Joanne had run out to the corner butcher shop for some cutlets, and Martine and Jacques were preparing vegetables and boiling potatoes. Richard brought up half a dozen bottles of wine from the cellar.

Before long they were back at the table eating and drinking with good appetites, prompted by the emotions of the evening. The conversation turned to the future. Joanne asked, "What are you going to do now, Richard?"

"I don't know. The paper said there's a lot of interest in my work. Are they selling?"

Jacques responded enthusiastically, "Very well. Even the more expensive pieces."

"Don't you think we should take advantage of this?"

Martine was shocked, "Oh, Richard! Take advantage of your criminal actions following the death of your good friend Raymond Crosatier."

"I didn't kill him!"

Joanne was intrigued, "What are you thinking, Richard?"

"I can keep on producing sculpture. You can keep on selling. No one has to know I'm still alive. You can say that you had a tremendous inventory of my works. Besides no one is going to count how many Rosendales you sell."

Jacques frowned, "But how can you live? You're a dead man. If any-one sees and recognizes you, you're arrested for fraud and maybe mur-der."

Richard turned earnestly to Martine, "Will you come and live with me in the south, in Saint-Paul-de-Vence?"

"Of course."

"I've been thinking about this a lot in the last four days. And I think we can pull it off. I'll of course have to leave Paris; too many people here who would be surprised to see me back from the dead. Last winter I spent a couple of days in Saint-Paul which has a large artistic commu-nity. It's a beautiful place. No one there knows me. I'll be able to work there. We'll leave tomorrow; I'll send you weekly packages of my latest works that you can sell; you can send the money to Martine."

Joanne asked worriedly, "What about your parents, Martine?"

"I'll think of something. I've decided I can't live at home. I need to travel. I've met a new man. They've always left me alone."

Richard's enthusiasm grew as he recognized his friends' gradual acceptance of his mad plan, "I'll have the freedom to create new works without having to worry about money. Living in Saint-Paul with Mar-tine. It all sounds heavenly."

Joanne again interjected a practical objection, "The interest in your work will gradually die down."

"In the meantime, we've made enough to live on, modestly, for a cou-ple of years."

Joanne was still worried, "We could all get into a lot of trouble."

Jacques, however, was increasingly tempted, "We could all make a lot of money, without hurting anybody, and without really doing anything illegal. We'd be just selling works of art, which are not stolen, and which are not forgeries. And we'd be helping out a good friend and a poor struggling artist."

Joanne gradually gave in, "I guess we should do this, but we've got to be extremely cautious. Richard, let's pretend that Martine, Jacques and I don't know anything about what you did to Raymond. And I don't think anyone would put us in jail for just knowing you're alive."

"Sure. Besides, when they finally figure out that Raymond is missing, I'm the only one who could possibly be in trouble, and everyone thinks I'm dead."

At that very moment, the door burst open, and a plainclothes policeman, Inspector Fabrice Pallini, pointed a gun at the three of them, "Richard Rosendale, you're under arrest for the murder of Raymond Crosatier."

CHAPTER 8

In the early stages of their new life of crime and sex, Olivier began to note the details of the thefts and of the rewards from those thefts in a journal. It was actually Claudine's idea; she reasoned that their thefts would necessarily be at infrequent intervals, and that a literate narration of them might continue to excite them between thefts. They read the journal to each other, like some couples might read pornographic literature to excite their passions. Here is the entry dated May 16:

"At 4:15 this afternoon, Claudine and I entered the Cluny museum determined to steal the crystal ball which was part of the treasure recovered in 1653 from the tomb of the fifth century Frankish king Childeric. These crystal balls, often surrounded by a gold mount, were found in the graves of many Frankish women and were assumed to be fertility talismans. The ball in the Cluny Museum was certainly not actually found in Childeric's grave but rather in a nearby and perhaps associated grave. It like many of the Childeric treasures was stolen from the Cabinet des Médailles in November, 1831, and later recovered when the police sent a diving bell into the Seine."

"We knew that the museum guard assigned to that room would immediately note its disappearance and sound the alarm. The trick was to substitute a fake crystal ball which would not be discovered until long after our departure."

"We also disguised ourselves in the expectation that the guard would eventually associate the stolen ball with the middle-aged couple and remember that the woman had sought to distract his attention for a time. Unlike our other thefts, this was not to be committed in the midst of friends. This had the advantage of making it certain we would not be immediately recognized, but the greater disadvantage that the guard would be much more likely to suspect the suspicious, unknown couple than our acquaintances for whom my reputation was a veritable shield of impunity."

"So, as a result of our disguises, when the guard eventually realized our guilt, he would describe to the police a mustachioed Englishman with a cane and a limp, accompanied by his deaf, red-headed wife. The red hair was of course a wig, and the deafness, suggested to us by Mme Grabois, served as the distraction we needed: while Claudine asked tedious questions whose answers she never got straight about objects on the far side of the room, I neatly substituted my clever imitation of the crystal ball—which Claudine had found at the flea market and which I had modified to match the drawing by the archeologist Chifflet reproduced in the museum's illustrated guide—for the real one which I slipped into the oversized pocket of my British slicker."

"In keeping with the medieval tenor of our theft, and the monastic heritage of Cluny, we decided, upon the successful completion of our caper, to act out a fantasy in which I was a robed monk and she a convent novice coming to me for confession. She had agreed that in exchange for the theft of the crystal ball she would act out any penance for her 'sins' that the good monk recommended and would invent some sins that might suggest interesting penances to be performed with the monk. The crystal ball played a central role in several penances."

The entry from the previous week was less detailed:

"Probably worn out by last night's activities, we could think of nothing more adventurous today than to steal an antique gold perfume bottle from a display counter at the Rouget Jewelry Store on the Avenue de l'Opéra. Claudine was particularly daring, taking the case practically in front of the salesgirl, and was amply rewarded this evening for her daring by forty-five minutes of stimulation."

Armed with this journal, which went on to narrate seven other thefts including Madame Dessailly's ruby and pearl bracelet, a Rubens still life featuring apples and pears belonging to a private collector, a miniature silver tea set from a home in Versailles, a set of gold cufflinks with pineapple motifs from a Royalist Notary, a gold antique inkwell from the home of the Minister of Public Education, and a diamond ring from Princess Poniatowski, Olivier paid a visit on May 25 to his friend and personal physician Dr. Emanuel Dutaut. Dr. Dutaut, who had studied with Freud in Vienna, was immediately fascinated by Olivier's account and journal and was eager to work with his old friend's new obsession.

"I see a definite pattern in the objects you have stolen; they tend to be works of art or antiques, the product of artisans or artists. There are clear feminine associations with all of them, as they are either feminine jewelry, or feature round or spherical motifs which suggest fertility or at least enclosure. Have you and Claudine discussed the nature of the objects you steal?"

"Yes, we do, consciously seeking interesting pieces which have artistic value."

"While unconsciously choosing pieces that have a feminine vulnerability. Are further thefts contemplated?"

"I suppose so."

"And why do you come to me?"

"The question is quite fair, since, as I have already stated, I have no guilt or regrets for the thefts we have committed and no fear of our being unmasked—or, to state it more accurately, the slight fear I do feel is greatly outweighed by the joy, the exhilaration, the sense of really living life to its fullest potential, which accompanies the thefts and the rewards."

"The truth is, Emanuel, that I sense we cannot go on in this way forever. Ignoring for a moment the actual criminality of our behavior, I am nonetheless concerned that our new attitude has altered our public behavior. Without our being unmasked for the crimes, there is still a real danger of compromising my position by the outward changes in our public personae. Little else interests or amuses me nowadays. My position, my social contacts, all my previous life seems less meaningful to me now. And yet I am rational enough to know that my future depends on my maintaining my professional and social reputation. I fear I may be sacrificing my future for a joyful present even though I am sure I will never be unmasked."

"Have you been aware of any loss of esteem, or any change in attitude, from your professional and social acquaintances."

"Not yet. I still maintain the persona they expect of me, that of the brilliant and eminently respectable Baron d'Anglade, but I sense that I am less and less willing to maintain that persona. I have begun to despise Baron d'Anglade."

"I fear this is indeed a very dangerous state of mind, a schizophrenic tendency which can do you great psychic as well as social damage."

"At times I am very distressed by this conflict."

"Of course you are!"

"Can you help me?"

"Yes, I can, most definitely. But this will require months of therapy. And must include the Baroness."

"That will be very difficult, if not impossible. She perceives no problem; on the contrary, she has never been happier."

"We can begin without her, but ultimately you will have to make her see that she is destroying you."

"How should I proceed?"

"Come back to me in a week. In the meantime, continue as you have."

"Are you advising me to keep stealing?"

"Since you are certain that you won't be caught, I think it would be prudent for you not to make any abrupt changes in your behavior. Latent schizophrenia, Olivier, is a very perilous and fragile state. We must do nothing to jar the emerging, pleasure-seeking component of your psyche."

"Your diagnosis, Emanuel, seems very menacing."

"You have come to me in good time, Olivier. Your condition will respond to classical psychoanalytic treatment…"

CHAPTER 9

The Ministry of the Interior, housed in the northeast corner of the Palais de Justice on the Ile de la Cité, overlooked the Quai de la Mégisserie on the right bank of the Seine. Michel deGrael's office, decorated in authentic Louis XV with Aubusson tapestries on the wall and floor, was brightly illuminated by four large windows recently cut through the thick stone walls.

On the morning of the same May 25th, while Olivier was hopefully consulting Dr. Dutaut, Michel was interrupted in his reading of the morning papers by his intercom announcing the unscheduled visit of Jean-Luc Saccard, Commissioner of Police. Saccard, the tall rugged replacement of the legendary and much regretted Félix Brochaine, had already begun to distinguish himself for his boldness, integrity, tact and icy intelligence. Michel greeted him with a smile.

"Good morning, Jean-Luc. And congratulations to you for the speed with which your inspectors wrapped up that silly murder of the journalist Crosatier and the Bank of France affair. I've just read the accounts in this morning's paper. Embezzlement is always a nasty matter; bank directors, no matter how prudent and honest their conduct may really be are always compromised in such matters. When the bank director is a political appointee, well...the possibilities of scandal are tremendously worrisome. I am sure that the Prime Minister is as grateful as I am that our friend Mervillle has been completely exonerated. The paper actually praises his conduct. I am convinced that the way in which your inspectors handled the matter, the speed with which the case was solved—as well as your tactful handling of the press—have saved us all a lot of embarrassment."

"Thank you, sir. I must point out that the Crosatier affair still has some unanswered questions, and that in both cases my personal role was small…"

"That may or may not be, but to the same extent that you take the ultimate responsibility for the rare failures of your police, you must also learn to accept graciously praise for a job well done."

"I am very grateful, sir, for your kind words. It is not, however, because of the Crosatier murder or the Bank of France affair that I have come to see you."

"Of course, not. Your exquisite modesty would have prevented you from coming here to accept praise. What can I do for you, Jean-Luc?"

"Sir, it is the recent series of puzzling thefts of jewels and artworks that I need to discuss with you."

"Oh yes, the so-called high society ring."

"That's it sir."

"In this matter, the success of your police has been less brilliant. The newspapers have still been patient, though they did report rather derisively the mistaken arrest of the unfortunate Englishman who had no trouble establishing that he was at home in London at the time of the Cluny theft of which your inspectors accused him…"

"Only after the museum guard had made a positive identification!"

"Yes, of course. At any rate, you know that I am sympathetic. Are we really dealing with remarkably clever professionals?"

"Yes, and no, perhaps."

"A guarded response. What do we know, Jean-Luc?"

"We have actually learned nothing for sure: the criminals have left no trace, no clues in the traditional sense. Our informers who have infiltrated most of the underworld's theft rings have found nothing; they report in fact that known traffickers in rare artworks are themselves baffled, that none of the recently stolen pieces has surfaced. All of this leads us to believe that not only are we dealing with an extremely intelligent

group of criminals, but also that their motive is not to capitalize immediately on the monetary value of the stolen treasures. In fact, it has been
theorized that their may be no financial motive at all."

"You mean, we're dealing with connoisseurs who steal art for their
own enjoyment?"

"Perhaps not that either."

"You are being very mysterious, Jean-Luc. Just what are you thinking?"

"It is not so much that I am doing any thinking, sir. In fact the theory
that I must expose to you, sir, well…it is not my theory, and I don't
think that I believe in it at all myself. I would be crazy to believe in it,
and yet when Renaud came to me yesterday with his idea, after rejecting
it and berating him, I couldn't get it out of my mind all night. I didn't
sleep at all. I decided that I had to let Renaud explain his theory to you."

"Very nicely presented, Jean-Luc. You have succeeded in creating a
damnable aura of mystery surrounding this theory, you have disengaged
yourself from all responsibility for the theory, and you have made me as
curious as hell to hear what Renaud has to say. Send him to me."

"I thank you, sir, for noting the successes of my preamble to Renaud's
theory. I have a fourth goal which I must meet before I can leave you
face to face with Roland."

"And what is that?"

"I must defuse the anger, the incredulous scorn and the mocking
laughter with which you will greet Renaud's accusation."

"Does he accuse a politically or socially prominent individual?"

"Yes."

"I see. You have done well, Jean-Luc. Very well done, Jean-Luc. After
having distanced yourself substantially from Renaud's accusation, yet at
the same time suggesting that you give some credence to it, you place
yourself as a shield between him and myself, to protect…both of you.
All right, Jean-Luc, it is time to tell me whom Renaud accuses; I admit
that I am prepared to hear anything and to receive any accusation without anger or scorn. Who is it?"

"Olivier d'Anglade."

Much to Saccard's astonishment, deGrael not only kept his promise, but showed not even surprise. "Go get Renaud."

"He's in the anteroom."

Summoned by Saccard, Inspector Roland Renaud entered uncomfortably. He was an old veteran of the investigative police force with several notable successes. Visibly humbled by the impressive surroundings of the ministry offices, Renaud looked for encouragement from Saccard.

"It's all right, Renaud. The Minister is not angry. He will hear you out even though you accuse a man who is not only socially and politically prominent, but who is also one of his closest friends."

At that introduction, Renaud lost any remaining traces of composure and gasped, "Closest friends!"

Saccard looked at him with an incredulous smile. "You didn't know?"

"No, sir. Perhaps I should withdraw...or resign...or..."

DeGrael stopped him with a gesture. "We are professionals, all of us, doing our jobs. Tell me your theory."

"I didn't know, sir. I'm terribly sorry. I knew I was dealing with a prominent individual, but I had no idea, I did not mean to accuse, I..."

"Tell me your theory."

"Yes, sir." Renaud pulled out a notebook and referring often to notes, occasionally reading a prepared narrative, told his story to his obviously interested audience.

"Our investigation has been going on since April, since reports began to come in of the disappearance of valuable jewels and artworks often under similar circumstances: most were stolen from private homes, no indication of forced entry, always just one object stolen. The Cluny Museum theft appeared to be an exception, and at first I was tempted to believe that that theft was unrelated to the others. But the nature of the object stolen fits the pattern, and then, well, it was the only theft in which we had something to follow up: the description of the English couple—obviously a phony English couple—provided by the museum guard."

"None of the stolen objects has ever turned up. Our informers have discovered no trace of any of them. The usual underworld sources of information are as baffled as the police."

"One tentative conclusion to be drawn from these facts is that the motive of the thefts is not money. This leaves the possibility that the thieves are collectors or working for a collector. But most of these clandestine connoisseurs are either officially or unofficially known; our inquiries among them have been fruitless."

"I started working on another hypothesis, trying to imagine an art thief or a group of art thieves whose motive may be neither monetary gain nor love of art. What could the motivation be? Your guess is as good as mine, but it seemed to me that at least part of the motivation for these thefts must be the satisfaction of baffling the police. We are undoubtedly dealing with an individual who finds in the morning paper's accounts of the police's befuddlement evidence of his own superior intellect, and who, aware that his crimes are apparently motiveless, takes a secret pleasure from the police's frustration. In other words I hypothesize as at least a partial motive a subtle vengeance against the police."

"We began to draw up a psychological portrait of such a criminal: we came up with the idea of an individual of unusual intelligence and arrogance who does not have all the power or wealth that he feels he should and in some way holds the police responsible."

"At about the same time I made a startling discovery. At first, only three of the burglarized individuals reported that they had held receptions in their homes in the days just before the theft was noticed, and very reluctantly suggested that one of their invited guests might be a thief. But when we made further inquiries we found that in every home in which a theft had occurred, there had been a large private reception."

"At our request, all of the victims very reluctantly submitted their guest lists to us. The names of several persons appeared on many of the lists—not surprising since we were dealing with a socially prominent elite group. But only one name appeared on all of the lists, the name of an individual who quite possibly meets the psychological portrait we had drawn and who could also match the description of the Cluny guard's phony Englishman."

"In fact, we had one of our police artists draw pictures of the man and his wife and then alter them with the elements of disguise and costume described by the museum guard. Just yesterday morning, the museum guard, when confronted with the altered portraits, identified them as the phony English couple. The altered portrait of the man bears also a remarkable likeness to the Englishman who had been erroneously arrested. As you already know, the couple is Olivier d'Anglade and his wife."

DeGrael's expression did not change throughout the narration. At its conclusion, he calmly asked Renaud how he planned to proceed with his investigation.

"This very evening, sir, there is a masked ball at the home of M. and Mme Alexandre Deslauriers in Saint-Cloud. M. Deslauriers recently presented to his wife a valuable diamond pendant. The d'Anglades will be there. With your permission, so will I."

DeGrael dismissed Renaud, and as the door closed behind him, the two stared at each other emotionlessly. After a few minutes of reflection, deGrael offered the opinion that there was at present no evidence on which to make an arrest.

"No, sir. Sir, should Renaud continue his investigation?"

"I would not want to interfere in an ongoing investigation. I want you, Jean-Luc, to be with him tonight. See there are no blunders or embarrassments."

"Of course. Anything else?"

After a few minutes of thoughtful silence, deGrael added, "You obviously want to know what I am thinking, but you are much too discreet to ask…It would undoubtedly surprise you to learn that I am somewhat preoccupied with…with thoughts of Joan of Arc."

CHAPTER 10

The interrogation cells of the Préfecture in Paris' sixth *arrondissement* are much the same today as when they were originally constructed in the mid eighteenth century. Electric lamps have replaced the original gas, but the stone walls, floors and ceilings are just as moist, foul smelling and oppressive as when Vidocq there interrogated enemies of the Restoration in the 1830s.

On the same afternoon of May 25, Richard Rosendale was led into Interrogation Cell 6B by a uniformed police officer, his hands and feet cuffed loosely. Inspector Fabrice Pallini entered a few minutes later, stared silently at Richard, sighed, and began in a slow, methodical voice:

"Now, Richard, I know you've been through all of this several times, but there are a couple of points we'd like to go back over."

"If I have to."

"You do. Now, you have stated and we have found witnesses to corroborate that you and the deceased left the Calumette about eight, that you had dinner at the Aristide, and then went around nine-thirty to the Café Rembrandt for 'a drink'. Is that right?"

Richard answered hollowly, "Yes, that's right."

"What did you and Crosatier drink?"

"At the Calumette I was drinking draft beer."

"How many did you have?"

"Three or four."

"The waiter says six."

"Maybe."

"And Crosatier?"

"He was drinking Pastis."

"How many?"

"About the same number."

"Right. And with dinner?"

"We had two bottles of red wine."

"And at the Rembrandt?"

"We were both drinking cognac. I don't remember how many."

"The waiter thinks you each had four."

"Maybe."

"Patrons at the Calumette overheard you shouting at each other, mostly in English. What was that about?"

Richard sighed again, "Oh, it was an old argument we've had a hundred times about the primacy of aesthetics and philosophy in the creation of art. He thinks…he thought my work was too cerebral. And I think that most so-called art isn't cerebral enough. There are too many brain dead artists making a big splash, people who wouldn't recognize a thought if you hit them over the head with it."

Pallini frowned, "And you actually get into shouting arguments about that?"

"Absolutely."

Pallini couldn't help reacting with a friendly shake of his head at Richard's obvious sincerity. He went on, "Now, I want you to recall once again everything that happened after you left the Rembrandt."

"As I've told you several times, it's all a little jumbled. I've never denied that I was very drunk!"

Pallini looked over his notes, "Six beers, probably a bottle of wine and four cognacs. I'm sure you were. Just tell me what you remember."

"Well, it was you who told me that it was just after midnight when we left the Rembrandt."

"Right, and you two had been shouting again."

"Raymond had gotten angry several times when I accused him of working for a fascist newspaper, of selling himself to the Right."

"I can understand that that might have made him angry."

"At any rate, from the Rembrandt, we walked to the Seine and then along the quais to the Pont Neuf. We walked onto the island, and since it was a beautiful night we decided to sit for a while in the little garden around the statue of Henri IV. Then suddenly, Raymond made a choking noise, put his hand on his chest and fell over. I rushed to him, pounded his chest, tried to revive him—clumsily, I was drunk, and I had never really learned how. I called out for help, but no one was around. Ten minutes went by during which I was sort of paralyzed, I didn't know what to do. He had stopped breathing, his hands were icy. I knew he was dead."

"At first I was amazed, then there was nothing: no panic, no sadness. I knew he had no family, no one to miss him, no one I should rush to inform and console. And then I thought about the movie, and the faked suicide. I was sure that Raymond himself would have wanted me to do it. So I changed clothes with him, put rocks and a wine bottle full of dirt into his pockets and rolled him over the low wall into the Seine."

Pallini looked over his list of scripted questions, "Didn't it occur to you that once the body was identified, you would be immediately suspected of murder?"

Richard grew thoughtful, "Not then. I certainly wasn't thinking clearly, but I thought everyone would assume it was me, and that the body would never be correctly identified. It was only the next morning, when everything appeared to me much more logically, that I realized I could be in serious trouble. Excuse me, but can I ask you a question?"

Pallini nodded, "Yes, you can ask a question."

"What made you people suspect that the body was Raymond and that I was still alive?"

"An anonymous tip. We didn't take it too seriously, but we decided to watch your apartment just in case. It paid off."

Pallini looked up from his notes, stared at Richard a moment, and then in a completely different, less official and clearly more friendly tone of voice, asked, "Rosendale, how long have you been in France."

Richard noted the change and relaxed, "I first came here as a student in 1928. I became a permanent resident in 1933."

Pallini went on in the same tone, "Why would an American who obviously isn't making a lot of money want to live in Paris?"

"I came here to study sculpture; there's no better place in the world to study sculpture than Paris."

"Why have you stayed? Couldn't you be earning a lot more money in the U.S?"

"Money isn't very important to me."

Pallini stared a moment then asked bluntly, "What is?"

"Art. And even despite my present lack of success, I don't believe there's a place in the world where art is more appreciated."

"What else is important to you?"

"My independence, my friends...intellectual conversations, ideas..."

Pallini dropped all pretense of a police interrogation, smiled briefly, then went on in a serious but friendly tone, "Look, Rosendale, I'm beginning to believe your story. I don't think you're a murderer. You did get into a shouting match with a guy who was later found in the river, but if you were really arguing about philosophy and art or the way a guy earns a living, well those subjects don't usually provoke murderous rages. I think you're weird, but I don't think you're a murderer."

Richard smiled ironically, "That's comforting."

Pallini's voice rose a degree and became once again official, on the record, "You did make a big mistake, though, and you could be in a lot of trouble for it. Where did you go after you dumped the body into the Seine?"

Richard repeated mechanically what he has already said dozens of times, "I wandered a long time, then fell asleep under Sully Bridge."

Pallini consulted his notes again. "And for three weeks you wandered around Paris living like a bum?"

"That's right."

Pallini closed his bulging notebook, took a deep breath, and with his eyes narrowed on Richard asked in a cold, serious voice, "Richard, now I want you to answer me honestly. At any time since that night, have you in any way been tempted to think, or have you had maybe just the beginning of the thought that perhaps, when you threw him into the Seine, Crosatier wasn't completely dead?"

At exactly the same moment, a short man nattily dressed in tweeds entered the Friedland Gallery. Jacques approached him, and smiled, "May I help you?"

The customer didn't hesitate, "I'm interested in Rosendale."

Jacques, who was no longer surprised by the growing interest in his imprisoned friend, started to guide the customer towards the rear of the gallery, "We have a few of his pieces. Let me show you."

The customer stopped him, "What can you tell me about him?"

Jacques frowned, "What do you want to know?"

"Did he kill Crosatier?"

Jacques looked at him with disgust, "No."

The customer smiled cynically, "You believe the story about Crosatier suddenly falling down dead?"

Jacques was not sure he wanted to continue this conversation with a stranger but felt an obligation to defend his friend, "Of course. Richard couldn't kill anybody. He's an artist, a very gentle man."

"If he's so gentle, why did he throw his friend's body into the river?"

"He was drunk. It was a crazy idea he had, to fake his own suicide."

The customer retorted triumphantly, "Drunk. Crazy. Doesn't sound like such a gentle artist."

Jacques grew increasingly irritated, "What do you know?"

"Just what I read in the papers. And believe me there's enough there to keep you busy for a long time. And everyone is talking about it. Rosendale has become a household word."

Jacques couldn't hide his dismay at the truth of the customer's observations, "What a pity!"

The customer smiled, "Can't be hurting sales."

Jacques had to agree, "Nothing could have hurt his sales. There weren't any before."

"And now?"

"People come in to see the few pieces we have. Some just ask questions like you. But lots buy. Yes, we've sold a lot of Richard's work."

"What do they go for?"

"The smaller ones for three thousand francs, the larger ones for five thousand."

"He'll be a rich man if he ever gets out of jail."

"He'll get out."

"The police think he's a murderer."

Jacques was growing increasingly tired of the conversation and tried to turn away, "The police are wrong."

But the customer put his hand on Jacques' arm, "The preliminary coroner's report showed Crosatier died of drowning."

Jacques pulled away, "If Richard says he had a heart attack, he had a heart attack."

The customer was emboldened by the sense that he was scoring points and winning the argument. "I thought Rosendale was a sculptor; is he a doctor too?"

"He knows a lot about medicine. Say, are you interested in buying anything?"

"Yes, I'd like to buy a Rosendale sculpture, this one."

"This one's five thousand francs."

The customer reached into his wallet and started peeling out bills "I'll take it."

Jacques picked up the sculpture and started towards the counter, "I'll wrap it up for you."

"Are you surprised I'm paying five thousand francs for this?"

Jacques didn't even look up from the wrapping process, "Not at all, since that's the price I just quoted you."

The customer crowed confidently, "The way I figure it, this piece is going to be worth twice that much in a few days, and ten times as much in a year, after he's convicted, and executed."

Jacques couldn't hide the disgust on his face, "Your guess is as good as mine."

"An artist who is also a murderer, well, that's bound to attract some attention."

Jacques' face flashed with anger as he retorted, "And I tell you that Rosendale is not a murderer."

At that very moment, Martine entered, in time to hear the customer's final words on the subject. "I just wonder if it's occurred to him or to anyone else if maybe the guy wasn't really dead when he threw him into the Seine. If he wasn't, well, that explains why the coroner says he drowned and it makes Rosendale a murderer—even if he didn't plan to kill his friend."

With that the customer picked up his package, turned to exit and politely greeted Martine on the way out.

Jacques looked at her apologetically, "I'm sorry you had to hear that."

Martine shrugged, "It's OK. I've just been with Richard. Jacques, he's beginning to wonder the same thing. He's really down, Jacques."

"Crazy business! Why did he throw the guy into the river if he wasn't sure he was dead?"

"He says he was sure, but now he's not. The second autopsy report shows that Raymond did suffer a heart attack. But it's not clear whether he died from the heart attack or from drowning.

Jacques shook his head, clearly troubled but adds, "At least there was the heart attack. So they can't say that Richard meant to murder him."

Martine agreed. "Richard knows that. He didn't plan to murder Raymond. But now he really wonders if Raymond was dead when he threw him into the river."

CHAPTER 11

Alexandre and Florence Deslauriers had purchased three years earlier a large rambling estate in St.-Cloud overlooking the Parc de St.-Cloud, with the express purpose of giving Florence the opportunity to indulge in her favorite pastime: giving parties. At least three times a year since moving in, she had invited the brightest and the best of Parisian society to lavishly catered soirées, usually organized around a theme. This spring's event, scheduled for May 25, a costume party, had been eagerly anticipated by the hundreds of friends and social hangers-on for whom the Deslauriers' parties were a welcome diversion from the standard tedium of beau monde entertaining.

Among the first to arrive were two sinister looking revelers disguised as hooded executioners who found themselves alone in a deserted hallway. The taller of the two, after carefully examining the hallway and its doorways, approached his confrere: "Any sign of them?"

"Not yet, but most of the guests haven't arrived yet."

"You're sure of your information that they'll be dressed as Scottish Highlanders?"

"Yes, we've been following the Baroness for two days. She had a seamstress in the rue Bonaparte make the costumes. She bought a bagpipe from a gentleman named Campbell who lives in Neuilly."

"We'll split up and circulate gaily among the guests. Find me if you see them. And no matter what happens, no overt actions unless I give the OK. I will remain anonymous in any event."

Renaud nodded and went out into the gardens. Both men were experienced at passing unnoticed. Time passed and the crowd of richly costumed revelers grew steadily. Eventually, Saccard wandered into the ballroom where a table garnished with caviar, smoked salmon, mounds of exotic fruit and a champagne fountain had begun to attract a group of revelers. He took up his station by a curtained doorway and watched as several masked guests entered from the left, among them the hostess, Florence Deslauriers, in a very low cut shepherdess dress, and her husband Alexandre dressed as a pirate. Olivier and Claudine in their Scottish costumes, he holding a bagpipe, followed the group but momentarily isolated themselves in a corner of the room, within sight but out of earshot of Saccard. Claudine complimented Olivier on his costume and bearing, to which he responded that the traditional approach to wearing a kilt was rather drafty. She raised her eyebrows and verified with a furtive hand that his dress was indeed very authentic. For the purchase of the bagpipe, Claudine had been directed by the Alumni Club of Edinburgh University to a Mr. Campbell in Neuilly. She did not explain to him that it was for a costume party, nor did she tell him that she was going to slit the bag and create a pouch in which to hide a stolen diamond pendant. Instead, she explained that it was a birthday present for her husband who had learned to play during a summer in Glasgow and who had often expressed the wish to take it up again.

Confident that they were alone, Claudine expressed her disappointment that Florence was not wearing her famous diamond pendant. Olivier responded that it was not exactly shepherdess stuff, and guessed that it must be in her bedroom. After admitting off-handedly that he knew his way around in there, he motioned to his wife to follow him to watch at the door.

Saccard, while totally unable to hear their comments, observed their behavior and guessed correctly at their intent. As he started to cross the room to follow them, he noted that Mme Deslauriers, who had just re-entered the ballroom, was now wearing her diamond pendant. In fact she pointed to it in response to an objection from one of her guests and exclaimed to their amusement, "Well, of course I am certain that there are fabulously wealthy shepherdesses in the world."

As Saccard abandoned his intention to follow Olivier and Claudine, he joined the guests who continued to crowd around Mme Deslauriers, expressing admiration for both the necklace and the incongruous costume which set it off admirably. Olivier and Claudine re-entered the ballroom after a quick, vain search of the master bedroom; their eyes were immediately drawn to the center of the crowd, to Florence's breast upon which the pendant was coquettishly displayed. Olivier's disappointed grimace gave way to his most charming smile as he and Claudine approached the group.

Florence spied her former lover Olivier, and called playfully for him to defend her, "Olivier, these silly people claim that shepherdesses do not wear diamond pendants and objected when I put mine on." Olivier raised his voice above the approving laughter from the guests, and responded gallantly to the challenge, "I assure you, Florence, that every shepherdess I have ever known had at least one diamond pendant. They all have rich lovers. There has to be some compensation for their difficult lot in life."

Sensing an opportunity to engage Olivier in the kind of witty repartee which had first attracted him to her, Florence assumed the role of foil, and ingenuously asked, "Is it watching sheep that makes their lot difficult, Olivier?" To which Olivier, who had already anticipated the question, quickly answered, "No, it's the rich lovers."

Florence sought to prolong the game, "Poor shepherdesses. But do you really think, Olivier, that sheep are better company than rich lovers?"

"While, of course, Florence, you and I are not in a position to know about either for sure, it seems to me that sheep are generally more faithful, less demanding and better physical specimens." The crowd which had shifted its admiration from Florence's jewels to the charming bantering of hostess and honorable guest greeted each new response with laughter and shouts of bravo.

Sensing the success of her evening, and wishing to maintain the spot-light for a few moments longer on herself, her costume, her pendant and Olivier, Florence pushed on, "But you do agree that it's appropriate for me to wear my pendant with this costume?"

Olivier, to Claudine's growing but concealed annoyance, allowed his gallantry to interfere with his own best interest and concurred with his hostess; with a gesture to her décolleté, he agreed, "Of course. It sets off very nicely your other jewels."

Florence giggled and asserted her authority: "How delightfully naughty you are, Olivier. Well, it's obvious that to satisfy everyone, I will have to wear it only half the evening. For those who don't believe in wealthy shepherdesses, I'll take it off right now. And I'll put it on for you later, Olivier. Alexandre, will you put this away in my armoire. I'll put it on again at 10:30." Applause and laughter greeted the resolution of the issue. Alexandre headed towards the bedroom with the pendant, while the guests flocked to the serving tables.

The evening was off to a charming beginning, which the mountains of food and fountain of champagne continued to nurture. Each bearing a glass of champagne, the two executioners, while exchanging nods and greetings with other guests, disappeared out into a hallway for a quick consultation. After expressing his admiration for Olivier's sang-froid, Saccard proposed that he would follow him and leave the surveillance of Claudine to Renaud. They returned to the ballroom and found that the d'Anglades had momentarily isolated themselves from the other guests. Claudine, noting the return of the executioners out of the corner of her eye, casually turned her back to them and in a low voice pointed them out to her husband: "Have you noticed the two hooded executioners? At first I thought that there was only one and that he was everywhere. I just now noticed that they're twins. They have a peculiarly menacing air about them."

Olivier responded that one of them seemed particularly interested in the bagpipe. "Very unlikely when you think about it: an executioner interested in a bagpipe." He proposed to look for some means to create a diversion and attract attention, which would permit Claudine to go

upstairs unnoticed to the master bedroom. He gave her a quick description of the room's layout and guessed that the pendant would be in an
unlocked jewelry case on the top left shelf of the armoire on the far wall
of the room.

As Claudine started to slip off, one of the executioners appeared
poised to follow her. Olivier quickly slipped out through a French door
onto a terrace and blew into the bagpipe. Eventually a horribly discor-
dant and loud sound emerged. The Deslauriers and several party-goers
including one of the executioners rushed to the terrace and came upon a
smiling but apparently embarrassed Olivier, "I'm sorry, Florence. I
thought I was alone here for a minute and that no one would mind if I
tried this thing out."

"If you keep that up, Olivier, you will certainly find yourself very
often alone."

Olivier gave the appearance of a man trying to turn an embarrassing
situation into a joke, "Anybody know how to play this thing? I could use
a lesson."

A guest dressed as an aviator came forward eagerly to Olivier's rescue,
"I used to play one of those in my youth. Let me try." The crowd's murmurs turned to admiration and eventually applause as he took the bagpipe and did a credible Scottish tune.

Olivier continued to play along, "Well, bravo! Do you mind showing
me how?"

The aviator explained that it was really not too hard. He put the bagpipe in Olivier's hands, showing him how to hold it. While this was
going on, Claudine slipped in from behind them, followed by Renaud,
went up behind Olivier, put an admiring arm on his shoulder, and
slipped the diamond pendant into the pouch of the bagpipe.

Renaud and Saccard had not missed a thing. Saccard nodded to
Renaud. When the lesson was over, and the guests had applauded Olivier's primitive rendering of a few musical sounds, Renaud removed his
mask and spoke authoritatively showing his papers, "All right, everyone,
stay where you are, please. I am Inspector Roland Renaud of the Surety

Police. I believe that a theft has been committed. Baron d'Anglade, will you hand me your bagpipe, please."

There were gasps and murmurs from among the party-goers, but no hesitation on the part of Olivier, who complied with a smile. "Certainly, Inspector. I'm surprised I didn't recognize you earlier."

Renaud explained his actions to the growing crowd on the terrace, "Believing that an attempt was to be made to steal Mme. Deslauriers' diamond pendant, I have been watching certain guests here this evening. I believe, ladies and gentlemen, that Mme d'Anglade took the diamond pendant from Mme Deslauriers' bedroom while our attention was distracted by the Baron's bagpipe, and as I watched just now, she slipped it into a pouch neatly sewn into the bagpipe. *Voilà*...." He pulled out the pendant, accompanied by exclamations from the witnesses. "What do you have to say about that, Baron d'Anglade?"

Without hesitating or losing his smile, Olivier answered, "Well, I must say that I am embarrassed."

"Embarrassed, sir?"

"You see, I had no idea that the Police were also aware of the plot to steal my good friend Florence Deslauriers' diamond pendant. Inspector Renaud, we belong to different, unfortunately often rival, branches of the government, but we both have the security of our country's citizens at heart. I received information from Justice Department informers that an attempt was to be made to steal the pendant. Since I had planned to attend this delightful event anyway, as I do every year, I undertook myself, with my wife's help, to watch over the pendant. I was perhaps wrong not to involve the Police."

"You will all remember that I tried to prevail upon Mme Deslauriers to wear the pendant, confident that her lovely neck was the safest place for it this evening." Murmurs of assent and admiration for Olivier's gallantry greeted his explanation. "When I saw that she was going to leave it carelessly in her bedroom, I instructed my wife to fetch it and bring it here for my safekeeping. I certainly congratulate you, Inspector, for your zeal and your skill. I had told my wife to avoid attracting attention while fetching the pendant. As she is rather inexperienced in such clandestine matters, I suspect that it was not too difficult for you to observe her actions. At any rate, since you are the official representative of the Police, I turn the pendant over to your safekeeping. And again, on behalf of Mme Deslauriers, I thank and congratulate you."

Amidst congratulations, laughter and exclamations ("Did he really take you and Claudine for thieves, Olivier?" "We are very grateful for your concern, Olivier."), the guests escorted Olivier and Claudine from the terrace, leaving Renaud and the still masked Saccard alone.

"I'm terribly sorry, sir. The first howls of the bagpipe distracted me long enough for her to get into the bedroom. I saw her coming out, but I could not possibly stop her for I was not sure she had the pendant. I was sure I had them when I saw her put the jewel into the bagpipe. The man is remarkable."

Saccard removed his mask and consoled his colleague, accepting his part of the responsibility for their humiliating failure. Quickly his determination returned, "I am of course convinced of their guilt and as determined as ever to unmask them. Let's not waste any time. They are certain to be here for hours yet; let's pay a little call on their apartment. In response to Renaud's raised eyebrow: "I have the Minister's approval to pursue this investigation with thorough care."

CHAPTER 12

Saccard and Renaud quickly left the Deslauriers' party, not unnoticed by Olivier, removed their costumes, and drove back towards Paris. In the car, Saccard explained to Renaud that the Minister, while not explicitly authorizing a forced entrance into the d'Anglade's apartment, had offered him generous discretionary authority. Normal Saturday evening traffic around the Arc de Triomphe, down the Avenue Marceau, and across the Alma Bridge, slowed them down very little, so that by 10:45 they were parked on the rue Barbet de Jouy, and climbing to the d'Anglade's apartment. Saccard had no trouble opening the door. Preceded by the light of their powerful flashlights, they entered the apartment and made their way into the large bookcase lined study. Saccard instructed Renaud to look around the master bedroom while he went through the bookcases and drawers systematically and examined various objects around the room.

After about a minute, Renaud returned with a bracelet and a set of gold cufflinks. "I've found a couple of objects which I believe match the descriptions of stolen items."

Saccard examined the objects which Renaud had brought him, checked in a little notebook he carried and placed the bracelet and cufflinks in his pocket. He went to a bookcase, uncertainly checked a few titles, then noticed **the** notebook stuffed amongst them and pulled it out. He started to read, flipping pages, totally absorbed.

Several minutes passed until Renaud re-entered and whispered breathlessly, "Here it is, sir. In Mme d'Anglade's closet, the missing Rubens painting, and a diamond ring which I believe belongs to Princess Poniatowski…" He noticed that Saccard was not listening, and didn't even glance up from the volume.

"What's that?"

Saccard finally looked up, "I don't believe it! A notebook in d'Anglade's own hand describing each of the thefts he and Mme d'Anglade committed. Listen to this entry, dated May 9: 'Last night Claudine and I were invited to a large reception at the home of the Minister of Public Education. We arrived at the party with no plan and not even a clear idea what we might find. Early in the evening I noticed the minister chatting with friends in his private study. I joined their circle and quickly spotted a gold antique inkwell on his desk. I didn't take it right away, but returned later with Claudine. We closed the door behind us without locking it, and while I put the inkwell into the opening of her evening gown, she knelt down and…' I think I'm beginning to understand, Roland!"

"What's that, sir?"

It was not clear at the moment whether Renaud's question referred to his superior's sudden enlightenment or to the scratching noise they heard, the unmistakable sound of a key entering a lock. Assuming wrongly that the Baron and Baroness had decided to return early from the party, and not wishing to confront them in the midst of their unlawful search, Saccard and Renaud dashed off quickly and noiselessly into the kitchen.

The door opened and the servants, M. and Mme Brunot, entered with their friends Philippe and Jacqueline Martin. M. Brunot assumed the attitude of a generous host escorting guests into his home, "While you're turning down the Baroness's bed, Claire, I'll take care of our guests. The Baron has some excellent cognac and cigars, and I'm sure he doesn't mind that I dip into them occasionally. They're out late tonight at a costume party in Saint-Cloud. They won't be home for a long time."

Saccard and Renaud, seated uncomfortably at the kitchen table and having heard Brunot's generous invitation, decided to try to wait them out.

Meanwhile, the festivities continued at the Deslauriers'. The constant attention that Olivier and Claudine received from the other guests, as a result of the near scandalous confrontation with the police, left them no opportunity to converse privately. Guests who had not been present at the actual event had heard differing versions of the police's unbelievable gaffe, and sought out the d'Anglades to hear authentic re-enactments of the scene. All of the commentary condemned the boorish clumsiness of the police and exalted the brilliance and tact of Olivier's handling of the situation. High placed guests threatened to bring the matter to the attention of the President of the Republic. Olivier and Claudine played down the affront, characterizing the incident as an excusable mistake.

Claudine, attributing her sudden fatigue to the excitement caused by the evening's event, begged Olivier to take her home early. Olivier protested, and urged her to stay for another hour or so, in order to satisfy appearances. When they finally did leave, it was well past midnight. The party was still in full swing; most of the guests had remained. Florence Deslauriers regretfully bid them good night. While the police incident had added excitement and notoriety to her party, and created an event which would be discussed for years, her concern that these two stars of the Paris social scene had received an insult in her home left Florence frustrated and disappointed.

Olivier and Claudine's first chance to discuss the incident occurred as they found themselves alone in their car. Instead of driving straight home, Olivier headed into the Bois de Boulogne, and sought out one of the deserted wooded lanes frequented by lovers and prostitutes.

Olivier sighed, "Our first failure, my dear."

"Yes," added Claudine, "and a rather narrow escape to boot."

"Inspector Renaud obviously knows who I am. What would have made him so brazen as to accuse us in public? And who is his masked accomplice?"

"I was really very careful, darling. I don't think he could have seen me place the pendant into the pouch unless he had been expecting just that."

"The same thought has been haunting me, Darling. We had better be careful in the future. At any rate, you performed admirably."

"And you were magnificent, Olivier. I truly enjoyed watching you perform and seeing the face of Inspector Renaud decompose. I am so proud of you." And then she added suggestively "We did succeed in stealing the pendant, you know."

"That's right. And then I graciously gave it back."

"I think we can consider the evening a success after all."

"That remains to be seen."

Back at the d'Anglade's apartment, the Brunots and Martins were seated around the dining room table, at around 11:45. Renaud and Saccard were still trapped in the kitchen, waiting with increasing impatience the departure of the freeloading servants, who had drunk a lot of cognac. The men had smoked several cigars. Mme Martin commented ironically that the Brunots were indeed fortunate to have such lovely masters who let them partake so freely of their cognac and cigars.

Mme Brunot snorted drunkenly, "Lovely masters indeed!"

M. Martin looked at her with squinted eyes, "What in the world do you mean?"

"I mean that the Baron and Baroness d'Anglade ain't all that they seem to be."

M. Brunot grew anxious at his wife's lack of discretion, "Now, Claire!"

Mme Brunot persevered, "Eventually the word is gonna get out."

M. Brunot shook his head disapprovingly, "Only if you start telling people."

M. Martin, whose curiosity was greatly aroused, encouraged her eagerly, "Come on, Claire, tell us what they've done."

At this point, Renaud tiptoed from the kitchen, into the adjoining study to survey the situation; he looked at his watch and the clock, and stopped to listen for awhile to the conversation which he found increasingly interesting.

Mme Brunot, emboldened by Martin's urgings, went on, "Well, some of the things that go on in their bedroom...I hear them doing it and talking about it in words that would make anyone blush."

M. Brunot at this point chimed in, in a falsetto voice imitating Claudine, "Don't you have any more in there for me, Olivier darling?" At which they all roared with laughter.

Mme Martin wiped the tears of laughter from her face: I don't see anything wrong with their enjoying themselves together."

At which M. Brunot chimed in with a conspiratorial air, "They've been stealing things too." This information was greeted with gasps of disbelief from the Martins. Brunot went on, "Here, let me show you." He went to find the notebook which Saccard had put into his coat pocket. "He must have found another hiding place for his notebook...It's a sort of diary he keeps and tells about things he's stolen."

M. Martin, still incredulous, blurted out, "Baron d'Anglade stealing! What the hell for?"

Which M. Brunot cannot resist, "So his wife'll service him!"

This indiscreet revelation brought peals of uproarious laughter. For several minutes, the conversation went on in the same vein, with the Brunots describing in graphic detail their employers' sexual adventures, some of which they had actually overheard, others gleaned from the journal. Renaud, who had heard more than he cared to, returned to the kitchen to report to Saccard both the detail of the conversation and the hopelessness of their being able to escape any time soon.

The conversation went on for another hour or so, when finally Mme Brunot noticed the time and grew anxious, "Henri, it's almost one in the morning; aren't you afraid they'll be home soon?"

M. Brunot acquiesced and almost immediately wrinkled his nose, "Did you light a fire, Claire?"

Mme Brunot started to dismiss the possibility and then noticed the smell that had attracted his attention. Almost simultaneously, they all turned around and saw smoke filling the study, pouring in from the kitchen. In drunken confusion, they got up, started yelling "fire" while gasping for breath, tripping over one another and shouting for help; eventually they ran out into the hall. It was none too soon for Renaud and Saccard who quickly followed, gasping with handkerchiefs over their mouths, and completely unnoticed in the confusion.

As they scurried to safety down the hall, Renaud inquired ironically of his colleague, "Did your instructions from the Minister include setting fire to the place?"

"It won't do much damage, and seemed to be our only chance to get out of there unnoticed. Now, let's go back in 'attracted by the noise and confusion.'"

At that moment Brunot returned with a bucket of water which Saccard, bumping into him in the hall, took from him and rushed back into the apartment, shouting, "Quick, a few more buckets and it will be out."

They were soon joined by a parade of other neighbors; eventually firemen arrived with a hose, and the remaining flames were extinguished. Saccard and Renaud exited calmly in the midst of the confusion with the notebook, the bracelet and cufflinks, which they stowed in their car, and then returned. Eventually the smoke stopped and the Brunots, Martins, other neighbors, the two policemen and the firemen congratulated one another.

M. Brunot, who was happy to take credit for discovering the fire, but still anxious about his unauthorized presence in the apartment, exclaimed, "I can't imagine who left that burner lit or why the curtain fell onto it."

M. Martin, eager to help his friend responded helpfully, "It's a good thing you were here so late! If you hadn't discovered the fire, the whole apartment would have gone for sure."

Mme Brunot chimed in, "As it is, just a few floor boards to replace, a little washing, painting, airing and there won't be a trace. But the Baron and Baroness are sure in for a surprise!"

After answering more questions from the firemen, they all left. Fifteen minutes later, however, Renaud and Saccard returned to the now quiet apartment, and stationed themselves in an alcove adjacent to the study. They didn't have to wait long; at about 1:30, Olivier d'Anglade came bursting into the apartment, followed closely by Claudine. He ran to the kitchen, then to the bedrooms, then to the bookshelf in the study. As he realized that the notebook and several stolen items were missing, a feeling of panic gripped him, but before he could imagine a course of action or articulate his dismay, Saccard approached him gently and respectfully, "M. d'Anglade, will you please come with us."

CHAPTER 13

On the morning of May 26, Richard Rosendale was surprised to be awakened at 6:30, as someone opened the door of his cell, and another prisoner was ushered in. The man was clothed in typical prison attire, but his bearing and grooming immediately suggested that he was not a typical prisoner. Tall, handsome, tanned and aloof, the new prisoner sat on the bed which was assigned to him, and slowly looked around at the meager furnishings, then stopped his gaze on Richard. An ironic smile formed on his lips, and he said, in a most polite and elegant tone of voice. "Good morning. Please forgive me for barging in on you like this, uninvited and unannounced."

Richard smiled back, impressed with the man's bearing, manners and apparent adaptation to his new surroundings. "Good morning. I am Richard Rosendale, the artist."

"The artist-murderer?" the stranger questioned politely.

"The alleged-artist-murderer," Richard responded even more politely. "And may I ask what high crimes you are allegedly guilty of?"

"Robbery."

"A common thief?"

"Oh, no, a very uncommon one. Allow me to introduce myself, I am M. le Baron Olivier d'Anglade, Chief Magistrate of the Paris Court of Appeals."

"My goodness! Not common at all."

"No. And despite my twenty years of activity within the French justice ministry, this is one perspective on it for which I find myself somewhat unprepared. Please excuse me if I seem a little distant or distracted."

"Certainly. May I ask if your incarceration here is perhaps a mistake, or a political maneuver?"

"Neither. It is totally justified. I have been on a crime spree over the last several weeks that has totally justified the actions of the National Police. I find myself impressed with their cleverness in unmasking me, their efficiency in processing my case, and the respect and gentleness they have shown towards me since my arrest. I have been allowed to be in frequent communication with my wife, who, as you might understand, is somewhat less composed than I am, and the attorney, who is representing me."

Richard hesitated, curious to learn more about the crime spree of his very dignified fellow prisoner, but not sure if he should question more. Since d'Anglade seemed willing and perhaps even eager to discuss his situation, Richard eventually gave in to his curiosity and politely asked for details of the Baron's crimes. The latter willingly provided ample details of the thefts themselves, equivocating however on the question of motivation, referring to a general thrill related to theft and the avoidance of detection, rather than to the sexual motivation and Mme d'Anglade's role. Richard listened sympathetically, marveling at the Baron's acceptance of his certain political downfall and possible prison sentence.

Quite quickly following the Baron's arrest, Michel deGrael had intervened, not on behalf of the Baron, but to protect Claudine. He made it quite clear to Saccard that while he would in no way interfere with the arrest and eventual trial of Olivier, Claudine's role must be ignored. Saccard and Renaud were the only two police officials completely aware of Claudine's role, and were sworn to secrecy. The servants were of course completely aware, but their silence could be gained through a system of rigorously applied sticks and carrots. There was also the real danger that the guests at the Deslauriers' party might put two and two together, understand that Olivier and Claudine had indeed planned to steal Florence's necklace and guess at Claudine's role in all of the thefts. On the other hand, it would be quite possible to maintain that Claudine herself had been unaware of Olivier's real intent to steal the necklace, and had innocently handed it over to him for safe-keeping. Saccard had magnanimously rehearsed all of this with Olivier, which greatly contributed to Olivier's peace of mind.

While at first panicked and distraught at the discovery of the journal and stolen items in his apartment, and by his subsequent arrest, and then horrified at the prospect of Claudine becoming a subject for scandal-mongers, he was now really feeling quite at peace. As his conversation with Dr. Dutaut had suggested, Olivier was tired of the charade and eager to see it end. Now it was over, and while his future was very much unclear, that didn't really matter. Even prison did not scare him; he had been assured that he would be treated well, that he would quickly be released on bail pending sentencing, and that his cooperative attitude since his arrest would surely lead to a short comfortable prison stay in one of the Republic's most luxurious prison estates. His political ambitions were of course ruined, but he had already begun to despise them.

And so he quite gaily told his story to Richard, bragging about the clever stratagems and disguises he had employed, and dwelling at great length upon the previous evening's vicissitudes, from his triumph over the police at the Deslauriers' party to his subsequent undoing by the police's discovery of damning evidence in his home. However, as he was not completely aware of the full scope of the investigation which had aroused Renaud's suspicions, he could not fully explain how the police had managed to tighten their net around him on that fateful evening.

Having concluded his tale, Olivier looked up smilingly at Richard, "Your turn. Did you kill the journalist?"

"No, of course not. I threw a man I knew to be already dead into the river. A serious act, no doubt. An illegal act, I suppose. But hardly one that merits imprisonment."

"Is there not some uncertainty as to whether he was really dead when you threw him in.?"

"In the minds of some people, that doubt apparently exists."

"But not in yours?"

"As you have been very straightforward with me, sir, I will show you the same respect, and share with you some additional details…"

CHAPTER 14

Before dawn on the morning of May 27, Olivier d'Anglade was little surprised to note that his cellmate was escorted from their cell and released pending further investigation. Their conversation of the day before had left little doubt in his mind that Richard would ultimately be exculpated of the more serious charges against him. Richard's situation, attitude and character had been more than a minor distraction for Olivier. Although totally different from the points of view of social condition, education, and lifestyle, he felt a deep kinship with Richard. He had warmly urged him to seek out his help and whatever protection he was still in a position to offer in the future.

Having been informed that he was being released from custody pending further investigation into the death of Raymond Crosatier, Richard agreed to remain in Paris and to check in periodically with the préfecture. As he left the building and walked out into the still dark early morning, he noted with some irony that he was being followed. He walked directly to the rue Bonaparte, which he followed up to the Pont Neuf, walked three-quarters of the way across the bridge, and jumped into the Seine.

Eight days later, in a scene hauntingly reminiscent of what had taken place just a little over three weeks earlier, Martine was sadly packing up her belongings in their apartment on the rue des Saints-Pères. There was a knock at the door, and she opened it, to let Jacques and Joanne enter, once again.

"Please come in. Let me get you some coffee and something to eat."

"Oh, please don't go to any trouble," Joanne gently urged.

"It's no trouble. There's lots left over from the funeral yesterday."

Joanne, seeking something to say, asked, "Where did it all come from?"

"From the people. It was stranger than the first funeral. People I never knew and who never knew Richard showed up after the funeral bringing food and flowers. I gave all the flowers and most of the food away." She brought out coffee and pastries; they sipped and ate as they talked.

Jacques shrugged his shoulders, "So, here we are, all over again."

Martine responded in a lowered voice, "All over again."

Joanne took her hand, "And once again, there's nothing we can do to help."

"Oh, you've been more help than you can know."

Jacques interjected, "We've got another check for you from the sale of Richard's sculptures."

Martine sighed, "I'd trade it all and a lot more to have Richard back again, even as frustrated and crazy as he was."

Jacques nodded, "A fake suicide publicity gimmick, and then a real suicide two weeks later, that really is crazy!"

Martine objected, "But when you think about it, it's really so logical. Because of the failure of his exhibit and that stupid movie, he fakes his suicide by disguising Raymond's body as his own. And then, when he realizes that he might really be responsible for Raymond's death, and facing prison and the awful barrage of publicity, who can blame him for really killing himself?"

Jacques agreed, "He maybe thought he was protecting us too."

Martine frowned, "What do you mean?"

"He was smart enough to figure out that they probably let him out of prison so they could follow him, and he didn't want to lead the police to us and get us involved in this faked suicide, murder conspiracy."

"I guess that's possible. Do you think that they let him out of prison just so that they could follow him?"

Jacques nodded and added, "And because there was a lot of clamor for his release after the autopsy report showed that Raymond really had suffered a heart attack."

Martine sighed, "Why didn't the policeman stop him from jumping into the river?"

Jacques shrugged his shoulders, "As he said himself at the inquest, that was the last thing he expected Richard to do. He was just supposed to note his actions and contacts and keep him under general surveillance within the terms of his release."

Joanne snorted incredulously, "And he wasn't supposed to keep him from killing himself?"

"He testified that it was so dark that he couldn't see the surface of the water from the bridge. He certainly couldn't have been expected to jump in after him under those circumstances."

Martine sat down in the middle of the kitchen floor, looking up at Joanne and Jacques, her back to the refrigerator, "It all seems so inevitable, as if the Seine was all the time waiting for Richard, as if it had been decided long ago that the poor artist Richard Rosendale would end up in the Seine. The fake suicide delayed the real one, but at the same time made it more inevitable. Richard tried to outwit his fate—the river—but it outwitted him in the end. And here I am, once again, packing up the apartment, talking to you about the horrible irony of Richard's death."

Jacques consciously changed the subject, "You're going to stay with your parents in Sceaux?"

"Yes, but they're really tired of all this business. They hardly knew Richard and have been astonished to see themselves quoted in the papers."

Joanne agreed, "We all have been. The press has really been having a wonderful time with this whole strange adventure."

Jacques smirked, "If Richard weren't dead, we could all be having a wonderful time too."

Joanne was sincerely indignant, "Jacques!"

"I mean an artist fakes his suicide, maybe kills his best friend, then really commits suicide, all in the space of a couple of weeks, and as a result, prices of his works increase tenfold, and his heir and agents become modestly wealthy."

Joanne saw nothing wonderful in all of that. But Martine sadly agreed, "Jacques is right. Richard would find this wonderful too. And his funeral, the second one yesterday, which we found so atrocious, well, Richard would have loved it."

Jacques smiled, "You mean Richard liked circuses?"

"Loved them."

"Then he would have loved his funeral."

Joanne gave in to the general feeling of bitterly ironic humor, "We certainly have become very famous, as well as wealthy, Richard too of course. I don't think the fame will last very long though."

Jacques agreed, "Oh no, by next week the press will have found some other scandalous affair, and we'll all be forgotten."

Martine interjected hopefully, "All except Richard! Who knows, there may be a Rosendale Museum some day."

Joanne sat down on the floor next to her, "Even if there is no Rosendale Museum, the world will not soon forget Richard Rosendale. He has achieved a notoriety that few artists ever achieve. Let's hope that his artistic reputation will one day be as great as his instant fame."

Martine smiled, "We'll never forget him. He's really done a lot for the three of us."

Jacques enthusiastically concurred, "The Friedland Gallery has sold a lot of art and has a lot of new customers. And you, as Richard's heir…"

Martine interrupted him, "The money really isn't important. Thanks to Richard I went back to school, and I'll probably amount to something some day. I certainly have a lot more self-respect. I've also learned a lot about art, and a lot about how to live life. Beneath his wild, crazy ideas and his pretentious, flamboyant way of talking, there was really a sensitive understanding of life and art, and how you can live one while being faithful to the other. Anyone who has known Richard has to look at life a little differently. He kept making me ask myself what's important and worth my attention. Ideas, art, friends—they're probably what he thought were the most important things in life."

Joanne added, as she rose, "Richard really did influence a lot of people in the same way…Well, good by for now, Martine."

Martine got up, actually feeling a little better, "Good-bye, Jacques and Joanne. Thanks for all your help."

Jacques gave her a tender hug and added, "You're welcome. We'll certainly be in touch. If there's anything…"

And then, for the third time in this brief narrative, the door of Martine's apartment opened unexpectedly, and, to the utter amazement and confusion of Martine, Jacques and Joanne, not only Richard Rosendale, but also Raymond Crosatier and another distinguished looking gentlemen whom they had never seen before entered quickly and furtively, closing the door behind them, and by their attitudes and gestures urging silence and patience as Martine screamed and fell to the floor.

CHAPTER 15

Jacques was the first to break the stunned silence after Richard and Joanne had finished tending to Martine, "What...?"

Richard jumped in, "OK. First let me introduce a new and good friend, Olivier d'Anglade." Three jaws dropped simultaneously, and finally Jacques blurted out, "*The* Olivier d'Anglade?"

After Richard's affirmative answer and polite but confused hand-shaking, Richard quieted his friends down so that he could begin his explanation: "It was while I was being interrogated that I first got the idea. Inspector Pallini was so good that for a while he had me believing that I had really killed Raymond even though I knew he was still alive. I actually felt bad about it. Then it occurred to me that another, a 'real' suicide, would be a natural thing for someone in my position to do, that it would get the police definitively off my back; and it would provide some excellent further publicity for the works of Richard Rosendale, which you may remember was the original motivation for all this intrigue."

Jacques expressed the general perplexity remaining: "Wait a minute; you knew Raymond was still alive, so whose body did they pull out of the Seine?"

"I don't know."

"But he was wearing your clothes."

"Ok. Let me back up. He was just a derelict we stumbled upon, poor fellow. Raymond and I were wandering along the quais, very drunk, when we found him…unquestionably dead, probably had been for days."

Raymond jumped in thinking he could help clarify the remaining confusion: "And that's what really got the whole scheme moving. We had talked about faking Richard's suicide. But even as drunk as we were, we were afraid it wouldn't work. And then we came upon this body. It seemed too wonderful a coincidence to pass up. So we put Richard's clothing on him and tossed him into the Seine. And then we fell asleep under the Sully Bridge until the next morning."

Richard chimed back in: "And then we got scared. A body with my clothes on and my wallet: once they had figured out that it wasn't really me, what if they thought I had killed him? But then we decided that maybe that wouldn't be so bad."

"What?"

Raymond explained: "A lot more publicity and no real danger. The real stroke of genius was to make the police think the body was Raymond."

Joanne asked the obvious: "How did you do that?"

Richard smiled and assuming a husky nasal voice pretended to pick up a telephone: "Hello, Inspector. I think you should know that Raymond Crosatier, journalist for the *Figaro*, is floating in the Seine this morning, and that he and his friend Richard Rosendale quarreled violently last night." "That's all it took! We knew a lot of people had seen us arguing."

Joanne smiled admiringly, "So you gave an anonymous tip on yourself."

"Right. I didn't expect the police to close in quite so fast after I surfaced. I was tempted to let you three know what was going on, but I never got a chance."

"And where was Raymond all this time?"

"I went down to Saint-Paul-de-Vence on vacation the morning after I was murdered. I followed events on radio and in the papers in case I had to be miraculously resurrected to save Richard's neck. I almost had to!"

Joanne expressed a concern and surprise that others shared, "And you were willing to stay dead, to give up your life as a journalist for the *Figaro*?"

"It wasn't really much of a life I gave up. I will admit that the decision was made a little hastily, that morning under the Sully Bridge, with a hangover. But it still looks good to me. I just sort of fell into journalism because I was looking for a job after I got my degree in comparative literature. I was a pretty good writer and I knew a lot about art—because I had hung around a lot with Richard and his friends—so they hired me as an art critic. But I really hated writing for the newspaper, especially that one. Raymond Crosatier the journalist can stay dead for a while yet."

"So what are you going to do?"

"I've always wanted to write a novel. This business has given me a wonderful plot. Of course the names will be changed to protect the innocent. While Richard is creating posthumous statues, I will write posthumous mystery novels. My first one will be entitled, 'Who murdered Raymond Crosatier?'"

Martine who had gradually emerged from her stupor, animated by the growing gayety reminded him, "I thought you were going to change the names to protect the innocent."

Richard put his arm around her and smiled, "And you think Raymond Crosatier is innocent?"

"In some ways, very!"

Jacques added admiringly, "You seem to have the imagination to be a good mystery writer, Raymond."

Raymond responded modestly, "In this business, Richard has really outdone me in creativity. The 'second' suicide was all his idea. It scared the hell out of me when I heard it on the radio."

Joanne frowned, "How did you do that, Richard? Why didn't you drown in the Seine?"

"When I was a kid, I used to be a competition diver and swimmer. I knew I could swim across the Seine even with my clothes on. Even on a chilly spring morning it was easy. The trick was to find a spot dark enough so that the policeman following me wouldn't see me swimming away."

"And then?"

Raymond went on, "Richard called me the next morning, incidentally relieving my anxiety about his reported suicide; I drove up to Paris immediately to pick him up, and we hid out for a week in a small hotel in Normandy, until yesterday when we came back to Paris for his funeral."

"What?"

"Yeah, I was there disguised as a woman. You three looked so upset I almost said something to you. The rest of it was wonderful. I even took pictures." Richard took out a small album which he passes around.

Jacques shook his head, "That's really crazy!"

"Yup!"

"And you really think you have nothing to fear from the police?"

Richard shook his head, "Our worst crime was to throw an already dead man into the river. And besides, Raymond and I are both dead as far as they are concerned."

Joanne asked ironically, "Are you planning to stay dead for a long time?"

Richard grinned, "Someday, maybe, I'll send Inspector Pallini a post card telling him what really happened. I figure that eventually people will forget about Richard Rosendale, and sales of his works will slow down. Then it will be time for him to come back to life and tell the real story...Or another one..."

While Richard and Raymond unraveled for their old friends the mysteries of the preceding weeks, their new friend, Olivier d'Anglade, had been listening admiringly, enjoying their happiness and camaraderie. They suddenly realized that in their joy and astonishment at the appearance of Richard and Raymond, they had ignored and neglected their distinguished visitor. When they finally turned to him, he very modestly assured them of his keen interest in Richard and Raymond's fate, and briefly and unashamedly summarized his own recent criminal activity and arrest. He added that shortly after the release of Richard, his lawyers had arranged for his release on his own recognizance pending a trial which would be at least two months in preparation. He was very pleased that Richard had taken advantage of his private phone number which he had confided to him while they were sharing a prison cell. He added with a certain humorous melancholy, "I truly believe that the Ministry of Justice would be grateful if I could disappear in the meantime. If you would allow me to travel with you to Saint-Paul, I think I have some connections that would be useful to you…"

Epilogue

On the evening of April 11, 1937, the dining room of the Hôtel Miramar in Vence was closed to the public in order to accommodate an elaborate private dinner in honor of the hotel's permanent residents, vaguely characterized in the prologue to this adventure, and whom we can now clearly identify as Richard and Martine Rosendale, co-owners and managers of the hotel, Jacques and Joanne Friedland, Raymond Crosatier, and the Baron Olivier d'Anglade, also co-owner of the hotel, whose initial capital investment had made the project possible.

Two of the village's finest restaurants had collaborated on the meal, which included appetizers of fresh oysters, foie gras, saucisson sec du pays, a main course of bouillabaisse and roasted pheasant, and a variety of local cheeses and pastries. The hotel's well stocked cave furnished the accompanying wines, but a special supply of champagne and Sauterne was also shipped in for the occasion.

The mood was joyous but partially restrained throughout the service of the meal. The celebrants drank multiple toasts to the success of the hotel, and the constant pleasures of their new lives, but the presence of the caterers inhibited their allusions to the adventure that had brought them together. Finally, after the cheese, pastries, and liqueurs has been laid out on the mahogany credenza at the end of the dining room, Martine dismissed the caterers, and latched the doors with a conspiratorial wink to the other diners.

The first to speak was d'Anglade who rose holding lightly the champagne glass that had hardly left his hand all evening, and with all eyes riveted on him addressed his new friends:

"I would like to take this opportunity to bring you up to date on my legal status and other personal issues which I know are of interest to you. Fortunately, the Police have relaxed the zeal which characterized their first investigations of my recent activities. The government has come to its senses and realized that the unraveling of these adventures is as much a threat to it as to me. The potential harm to my friend and mentor deGrael and through him to the government itself—at a time when that government finds itself confronted by enemies outside our borders and growing internal political pressures—was far too considerable, and the too public attempts to bring me to justice had to cease immediately. There was also a little judicial discomfort with the police's illegal search of my apartment. This was a firm basis for prolonged negotiations throughout the winter involving my very able attorneys, negotiations which were founded on my eagerness to make full restitution and then some. Ultimately the negotiations included a considerable but manageable dent in my personal fortune, and a virtual banishment from the city of Paris. These negotiations are now concluded. I am not exactly a 'free man,' but rather a non-existent one."

"My efforts to protect Claudine have been completely successful. She will continue to live comfortably in Paris, surrounded by her friends and admirers there. She is a chastened and wiser woman, made much more appreciative of the many advantages her station in life offers. We have seen each other frequently, which is the reason for my nomadic existence over the past months. We have visited together European capitals, and will undertake together later this spring a trip to America. She has told her friends that I am still a trusted government aide, charged with missions around the globe, and they believe her."

"Richard, Martine, Jacques, Joanne and Raymond, my deepest thanks to all of you…When I consider the revolution in my life, when I compare who I was a year ago with who I am now, I am both humbled and exhilarated by the contrast. Your friendship and support have been of the greatest importance to me. I consider this beautiful hotel my home, and you my closest friends and neighbors."

As he sat down, Raymond Crosatier rose, also with a champagne cup in his hand. "I can only echo Olivier's words: 'When I compare who I was a year ago, with who I am now, I am both humbled and exhilarated by the contrast. Your friendship and support have been of the greatest importance to me. I consider this beautiful hotel my home, and you my closest friends and neighbors.' I wish merely to add that my newspaper long ago gave up trying to determine whether I was dead or missing, and presently doesn't care whether I am dead or missing. I have found joy, liberation, and some growing success as a freelance writer. I have found my greatest literary satisfaction in a work which is destined to be released only when those of us involved in it no longer can be harmed by it. It is a story that needs to be told—when the time is right. Thank you, friends."

Joanne and Jacques Friedland each made short awkward speeches, thanking their friends and extolling their new lives. They still maintained an active presence in Paris. The accelerated sales of Rosendale statues in Paris had permitted them to open their second gallery in nearby Saint-Paul, which was also doing a brisk business specializing in contemporary painting. They had signed an exclusive agreement with Marc Chagall.

Martine stood up with Richard, blushing at the applause and hurrahs in sincere tribute to the success of the Miramar. She declined to speak, but beamed proudly at Richard as he tried to finds words that reflected their happiness:

"Dear Friends, who would have thought, following that disastrous gallery opening just a year ago, that so many things could happen so quickly to make us rich and happy? I can only conclude that some magic genie has taken us under his wing, protecting us from our own mistakes, and guiding us towards this truly enchanted spot tucked between the Alps and the Mediterranean. I am not sure what the future will bring. Surely world events are ominous and disturbing. But I can't help feeling that together and here we can weather any storms, ride out any tempestuous seas, and sail steadily towards the unknown horizon that beckons. I am very grateful for Martine's love and support, and for her remarkably successful management of the Hôtel Miramar project which Olivier entrusted to us. I have found the freedom to continue to create, no longer fettered and frustrated by poverty and by the public's incomprehension, no longer alone…"

Richard's speech of course went on, almost beyond the attention span of his enthusiastic listeners which included this sympathetic chronicler, and certainly beyond any further indulgence one can expect from readers who have had the kindness to stay with us this long. Suffice it to say that the six friends celebrated far into the night.

0-595-65839-3

Printed in the United States
1311100001BA/142-168

9 780595 658398